Rufus and the Weed Man

Rufus and the Weed Man

Tim Brown

RESOURCE *Publications* · Eugene, Oregon

RUFUS AND THE WEED MAN

Resource Publications
An Imprint of Wipf and Stock Publishers
199 W. 8th Ave., Suite 3
Eugene, OR 97401

www.wipfandstock.com

PAPERBACK ISBN: 978-1-7252-7252-1
HARDCOVER ISBN: 978-1-7252-7253-8
EBOOK ISBN: 978-1-7252-7254-5

01/13/21

This book is dedicated to my father, who knew how to tell me to change my ways and make me think it was my idea.

Contents

1

Pikers

THE SCAR OVER ADAM Thompson's right eye was an ever-present reminder of his run-in with the Hudson brothers and was also the focal point of a storytelling game he played with his grandchildren. William was five, and Susan was almost three when Adam came home with a wounded forehead. The kids were curious about his wound from the beginning, and from the beginning, Adam told them stories instead of the truth. And, even as the cut healed and became a less noticeable scar, the grandfatherly foolishness continued.

"What happened to your head?" William asked.

"Your grandma hit me with a frying pan."

"Your grandpa is full of prunes," Connie, his wife, interrupted.

"What are prunes," William asked.

"I simply meant that I did not hit your grandpa with a frying pan."

"Then what really happened?"

Adam lowered the footrest on his recliner, put his feet on the floor and his hands on his knees, and said, "William, here's how it happened. I was in the woods hunting mushrooms when I heard a threatening snarl come from a nearby tree."

Adam stood up and walked slowly through the woods toward William. "I looked up, heard a loud and frightening shriek, and saw a fifty-pound bobcat jumpin' straight at me out of that tree."

Adam jumped at William with clawed hands and a full-throated growl. William's eyes widened. He giggled. Then laughed hard.

"His claws were as long as my thumb and razorblade sharp. His teeth flashed. I ducked but not fast enough. One of those deadly sharp claws sliced my forehead as he screamed by. I yelled, 'Stupid bobcat! Get out of my woods.' That darned bobcat ran like his tail was on fire and didn't look back. I guess I musta scared him pretty good."

William loved the story, even if he knew his granddad was fibbing. The story did more than satisfy William. It started a story-telling habit that included the entire family for a time.

If the kids were around, someone would ask, "Hey, Grand-dad, how'd you get that dent on your forehead." Then Adam would come up with another outlandish story. Connie finally asked him when he would tell the kids the truth.

"Those kids will eventually learn how nasty people can be, but they're not going to learn it from me," he said. Besides, I've become an excellent storyteller, don't you think?"

"Yes, you have."

Fibbing was Adam's way of turning a dangerous and com-plicated encounter into fun. The rest of the family encouraged his off-the-cuff fiction. Family gatherings were not complete unless someone asked him to explain his scar. If the kids forgot, usu-ally their dad, Mike Thompson, would do it. "Hey, Pop," he'd say. "That's a wicked little scar on your eyebrow. What happened to you?" With that, Adam would spin another tall tale. They all loved to hear him talk. Mike's wife, Molly, thought Adam should become a professional storyteller, maybe a writer or something.

"No, no, no," Connie said. "The job he has now is just fine."

She enjoyed their newly found stability too much to consider another change. Adam had switched jobs often over the years. He was never fired. He was a bright, congenial man who became bored and moved on, which is why everybody knew him, and most people liked him. It's also why he was recruited for his current job as noxious weed supervisor. He was the Nebraska Department of Agriculture's weed man in Fredrick County.

Noxious weeds are invasive species that can cost farmers and ranchers millions of dollars each year. They reduce yields and poison livestock and wildlife. Left unchecked, the fast-spreading biological litter can occupy vast stretches of property, making it totally unsuitable for agricultural purposes. Backed by both federal and state legislation, Adam's job was to find noxious weeds and advise landowners to eradicate them. If they didn't comply, the state did the job at the farmer's expense. And fines could be imposed, although it seldom came to that.

Adam saw himself as an educator and friend rather than an enforcer. He was two years into his new job, which he began in 1985. He scoured the countryside in his official-looking white pickup, spotted the troubling weeds, and approached the farmers with authentic friendliness. His easygoing manner worked well. After learning of their problem from this unassuming, pleasant man, most farmers were glad to destroy weeds that would harm their cash crops and livestock. He enjoyed the job and considered it a late-life blessing. "I'm outside all day talking to people. What could be better than that?" he asked.

Frederick County is one of the largest counties in Nebraska. It's a 770-square-mile rectangle with a population of just over 1,500 rural residents and 5,000 people who lived in his hometown of Spring Valley. Andrew understood the size of the county when he took the job; however, he didn't realize what a dissimilar assortment of people lived within its borders. There were a few malcontents in Spring Valley, but most of the people who lived there were friendly and welcoming. Adam learned that routine friendliness could be scarce in the more remote parts of the county, and that was especially true during the summer of 1987 when a trip to the hill country left him with a scar and set off a series of events that held sway over his life for months to come.

He packed an overnight bag and drove sixty miles north into hill country. He seldom was gone overnight but was always prepared if he needed to be. He pulled into a remote little village called Snyder, located in a sparsely populated corner of Frederick county, which Adam had never visited. Snyder was little more than a two-block main street with a small grocery store that doubled as a post office, a junky antique store, a Shell gas station, a tavern, and the Snyder Cafe. He stopped to buy gas and to ask how far it was to Pike County. His responsibilities only went to the Frederick County line.

Adam approached the attendant, who sat behind the counter reading a Spider-Man comic book. "Say," he asked, "do you happen to know how far it is to the county line? Pike County is the next county up, isn't it?"

The sour young man looked up, slowly stood, and took Adam's credit card. He ran the card and said, "North seven miles." He glanced outside and noticed the Nebraska Department of Agriculture seal on the door of the pickup, and that was the last three-word sentence he uttered.

"Straight up Highway 72?" Adam asked.

"Yup."

"Mostly pasture up there, I guess?"

"Yup."

"You live here in Snyder?"

"Yup," the young man said, handed Adam his credit card and a receipt, sat down, and returned to Spider-Man.

In need of a little more conversation and aware of the stultifying influence of his pickup, he drove a half block down the street and parked in front of the antique store. Then he walked another half block to the grocery store and went in. He shopped the snack aisle and picked up Beer Nuts and Cheetos and placed them on the counter in front of a middle-aged woman with heavily teased, auburn hair, who was on the phone. She cut the call short and flashed a quick, compulsory smile.

"Hello," the lady said. "That going to do it for you?"

"That should do it. Though maybe you could help me with directions," he said, behind his disarming smile that was devoid of malice.

The lady asked, "Where ya headed?"

"How far's the county line?"

"Just up the road, about seven miles."

"Mostly pastureland up there?

"Yeah, mostly. There is one farm a few miles up. Belongs to the Hudsons. But if you ain't a relative, you should just keep driving. Truth be known, although they live in Frederick County, they're Pikers through and through."

"I'm not sure I know what you mean," Adam said.

"Sorry, I forget that not everyone knows that word. Pikers are people who live in Pike County. Now, it ain't true of everybody who lives there, but there's a lot of ne'er-do-well outlaws up there. They'll cheat ya all day long and then laugh at you when you find out what they done. We call them Pikers down here." Then she stopped talking, realizing that she didn't know her customer well enough to be so gossipy, although he did seem to be a very nice man.

"Interesting," Adam said. "I will steer clear of the Pikers if I can. Thank you now." He started to leave and then turned and asked, "You said the Hudsons? That means there's more than one of them?"

"Three of 'em. They're brothers. And if you see one of 'em, you can be sure the other two ain't far behind. They shop in here sometimes. I'm nice to 'em, but I'm always glad when they leave. If they steal a pack of gum, who cares? I just want to be rid of them. I wouldn't fool with them if I was you, especially if I was drivin' a truck like yours."

"In a truck like mine?" Adam asked. "Did you see my truck?"

"My cousin owns the antique shop. He don't miss much."

He nodded, picked up his snacks, left the store, and steered his pickup straight up Highway 72 toward Pike County. He wondered if someone would call ahead to tell the Hudsons he was coming. After he had driven about four miles north, he saw the mailbox to the right side of the road. It was mounted on a wrought iron base shaped like an H. White lettering on the black mailbox read Hudson.

He slowed his pickup, noticed the dense growth of Japanese honeysuckle and black knapweed blanketing the road ditch and jumping the fence into a sparsely planted oat field. He turned in. The house sat off the road about an eighth of a mile, so there was time to turn around if he chose to do so. He didn't. He drove ahead through an open gate and over a cattle guard, which was a series of pipes placed across the road over a two-foot-deep ditch. The pipe bridge keeps cattle on the right side of the fence because they understand that if their leg slips between the pipes they'll be stuck or injured. A vehicle, however, can easily pass over the bed of evenly spaced pipes. As he drove across the cattle guard, it rattled. Cattle guards are usually embedded in concrete, which makes them rock solid. This one seemed oddly temporary. And there wasn't a cow in sight.

He drove another fifty yards up the dusty lane. The billowing dust cleared as his tires crunched on the gravel driveway in front of the house. The gravel seemed fresh, but it was the only thing that was fresh. The two-story house needed paint, the sidewalk was crumbling, and the screen door was off its top hinge. The house appeared to be abandoned. The only possible sign of life was the dented fender of a red bicycle, which protruded from behind the overgrown bushes. If the Hudsons were home, they knew he had arrived because of his tires on the noisy gravel. He sat in his truck for a few minutes, partially completing the noxious weed citation. It was a preprinted form. He needed only the landowner's name and address and the name of the offending weeds to complete it.

A heavy-set man in overalls opened the door and peered through the sagging screen. "Help ya?" he asked.

Adam got out of the pickup. "Maybe so," he said. "I'm Adam Thompson, the noxious weed supervisor for Frederick County. I'd like to talk to you about your weeds. Getting rid of some of 'em could sure improve your crops and protect your livestock. Put a little more money in your pocket. Do you have a moment? It won't take long."

"Who's out there, Harley?" asked a raspy, angry voice from the dim room behind the sagging screen door.

Harley spoke over his shoulder toward the angry voice, "Don't know for sure. It's some guy worried about our weeds."

"Who thinks we're growin' weed?" the unseen man shouted.

With that, a big, balding man brushed past Harley and burst through the screen door, forgetting about the broken hinge. The sagging screen door slammed askew against the side of the house.

"We ain't growin' weed, and we ain't cookin' meth. Now who in the hell do you think you are accusing us of breaking the law?" the enraged man shouted. "Now, get your goddamned government truck off my property before I lose my temper and get my gun!"

Adam stood on the fragmented sidewalk, directly in front of the house. He had one foot on the porch's first step, a safe distance from the irate man. He took his foot off the step, raised both hands, palms out, and said, "Wait, wait, wait. I said nothing about marijuana or meth. What I said was, I have some ideas for you about controlling your weeds and improving your crops. I'm with the Noxious Weeds Commission of Frederick County."

"That's true," the first man said, after stepping onto the porch behind his fire-breathing brother. "Least, that's what he said." The men were bookends. Both had several days' growth of salt-and-pepper beard. Both wore overalls, sweat-stained T-shirts, and worn-out work boots. Both had bulging torsos, although it was difficult to tell where the barrel chests stopped and the potbellies began. The loud one seemed to be a little older.

Adam extended his hand. "My name's Adam Thompson. I live down in Spring Valley, and I don't get up here very often, and, by the looks of the noxious weeds invading your oats, maybe it's a good thing I came when I did. I'd love to talk with you just a few minutes about how to get rid of them."

The man didn't shake his hand. He just looked straight at Adam and said, "My name's Rufus Hudson. This here's my brother Harley. We don't get much company up here, especially from the government." Rufus calmed a little. "So, you think I got weeds in my oats, huh? What kinda weeds ya say? Noxass? What kind of weed's that?"

"That's noxious. Means weeds that will harm your crops and your livestock."

"You don't say." Rufus paused and looked hard at Adam. No smile. No frown. Just a blank stare. Then he said, "Okay, you got five minutes. That's all. Step in and start talking."

Adam would have preferred to open his three-ring binder on the hood of his pickup and tell his story under the clear blue sky, but he thought better of it. Rufus had shown himself to be a very volatile man, and because he had gone from seething hot to cautiously warm inside of a minute, Adam decided not to press his luck and went inside.

"Have a seat," Rufus said, motioning to an old divan shrouded with a badly stained slipcover. The house smelled like day-old bacon grease and burnt toast. An orange cat with an oozing eye stalked about the room and finally jumped atop a tall, empty bookcase. It stared down at them through its one good eye. All three men occupied the couch—Adam in the middle, with the Hudson brothers on either side. It was awkwardly snug, but there was no other place to sit. The Hudsons were big, unwashed men. Their foul scent blended with the household odors and encouraged him to make this his shortest presentation ever.

"Harley, tell Ricky to get to work," Rufus said. Harley got up and left the room. Adam heard an outdoor bell clang three times. Harley came back and sat down a little too hard, causing an uncomfortable swell of broken springs and clumpy padding to undulate through the dilapidated couch. Once they were again settled in, Adam looked at Rufus for his approval to open his binder and begin.

"That bell's for our brother, Ricky. He's got work to do, and if we don't tell him when to start, he'll never do it on his own. Sorry for the interruption," Rufus said. They heard the popping sound of a tractor starting and then pulling away toward some preassigned task.

Although he was sandwiched between the two brothers, he gave most of his attention to Rufus. He turned binder pages as quickly as he could without appearing to be hurried. He slowed only to emphasize the damage the two noxious weeds he had seen on their property could do and to suggest the appropriate chemicals to deal with them. Giving the Hudson brothers a written citation for their noxious weed violation was a considered decision. Of course, it would have been better for their oats if he had, although probably not better for him. He decided not to formalize the complaint with official documentation.

He slowly closed the binder and placed his palms on top of it. "So, if you have any questions, call me at any time." He took two business cards from his shirt pocket and handed one to each brother. "I'll check back in a couple of weeks to see how you're doing on those weeds. And, unless you have some questions for me right now, I'll quit bothering you and be on my way."

"Well, learn something new every day, don't ya? Noxass weeds. Well, I'll be damned," Rufus said. "Maybe next time you're here, we can smoke a little weed!" Rufus and Harley both broke into hysterical laughter. Adam joined them with a well-timed, believable chuckle, which was more a measure of his relief to be leaving than it was an acknowledgment of Rufus's absurd joke.

The noxious weed supervisor for Frederick County thanked his guests for listening and hurried to his pickup. He threw the three-ring binder on the passenger's seat beside the unopened packages of Cheetos and Beer Nuts, started the engine, and waved goodbye. As he drove away, he checked his rearview mirror and noticed something written in the dust on the back window. It was just two words: The Barn. It made no sense. The only thing that made sense was to leave the Hudson place as quickly as possible. So, he drove.

He drove just a little too fast. Then he remembered the cattle guard and slowed the vehicle, but not enough. The dusty, white pickup slammed into a two-foot-deep ditch no longer covered by the cattle guard's piped grate. Its front wheels dropped and hit the trailing edge of the ditch straight on, and the pickup bounced two feet into the air. The vehicle's forward movement continued, and the back wheels hit the ditch and returned the favor. One more devastating bounce and the pickup came to a dusty stop on the far side of the cattle-guard trench.

In his haste, he had forgotten to fasten his seat belt, and his pickup's abrupt drop sent him, the binder, and his unopened snacks airborne inside the cab. The first bounce caused his head to hit the ceiling. The second thrust him forward toward the windshield, but the rearview mirror stopped him and gave him a painful a one-inch gash above his right eye. The mirror was knocked from its mount. He sat for a moment to let the dust settle and to gather his wits. He knew he was cut. His blood was warm on his cheek and bright red on his light blue shirt. He grabbed a clean T-shirt from his bag and pressed it hard against the wound, then got out of the truck and examined what he had hit. It was immediately clear what Ricky's preassigned task had been. He pulled the cattle guard's pipe grate from its moorings so that the ditch beneath was fully exposed. The rack of pipes rested on an eight-foot track to the right of the road. He looked back at the house. The Hudson brothers stood on the front porch laughing, waving, and high-fiving.

He seldom swore. This time he did. "Low-life, bastards!" he yelled at the top of his lungs. He got back in his truck and carefully tucked the T-shirt under his cap and against his wound. His hands were free to complete the noxious weed citation. He tore off the original and placed it in their mailbox on his way to the main road. His copy, complete with a bloody thumbprint, was stored in the pocket of his presentation binder. Rufus, Harley, and Ricky Hudson were served.

Adam headed back to Snyder, holding his T-shirt against his forehead. He knew that head wounds sometimes seem more severe than they are. Still, he wanted to make sure he wasn't hurt worse than he felt. He stopped at the grocery store because he didn't know where else to go. He walked in, keeping pressure on his wound. The lady with the teased, auburn hair took one look at him and said, "Oh my God, what happened to you? Don't tell me you stopped at the Hudson's place."

"Sorry to say, I did. Is there any place in town to get a stitch or two?"

"Well, let me see," she said. She took him by the arm and ushered him behind her counter. She sat him down in her well-worn, wooden desk chair next to the cluttered desk and the telephone.

She gently clasped the back of his hand, moving it away from the wound. The T-shirt came with it.

"Yes, sir, that needs a little attention," she said. The bleeding had almost stopped, but it was severe enough to need stitches. She looked up as she heard someone enter the store and disturb the dangling bell that hung over the doorjamb. It was her thirty-year-old cousin from the antique store. He shifted his Brad's Antiques cap to the back of his head as he approached.

"What's up?" he asked. He'd seen the state pickup parked in front of the grocery store and noticed its driver enter the store with a bloody rag held to his head.

"Well, Bradly, we got ourselves a wounded man here. Run over to aisle two and get me a box of square bandages and a small tube of Neosporin. I've got some peroxide over here under the counter." She returned her attention to Adam.

"This'll be very temporary. Where you from?"

"Spring Valley."

"That's more than an hour away. Be better if you could get fixed up before then. We'll call over to Doc Olsen to see if he can see ya. He's in Elwood. That's only about thirteen miles west on 48. Kinda out of your way, but a wise trip, I think."

Bradly delivered the bandages and the ointment and sat on the edge of the counter to watch the doctoring. "So, what happened to ya?" he asked.

"Hit a bump in the road and cracked my head against the rearview mirror," Adam answered, being careful not to offer too much information to the unintroduced man.

"Must have been quite a bump," Bradly said.

"Yes. Should have watched where I was going, I guess." Avoiding the inquiring man's attention, he spoke to the lady. "Ma'am, you've been very good to me. I don't even know your name. I am Adam Thompson. I'm the noxious weeds supervisor for Frederick County. What's your name?"

"I'm Kathy Burns. This here's my cousin, Bradly Parks. He owns the antique store next door. Now, lean back in that chair so I can get at ya." He bent his head backward and laid back in the chair so that its ancient springs were fully extended. She walked around him and cushioned his head against the crook of her elbow.

She blotted the wound with a peroxide-soaked tissue, and said, "Bradly, open the ointment and hand it to me. Then strip the back off the bandage and hand it to me when I'm ready." Her cousin did precisely as he was told.

Kathy squeezed an even line of ointment into the wound and closed it with finger pressure on both sides of the ragged cut. Brad handed her the bandage, which she placed gently over the wound.

"That should hold ya, at least until you get to Doc Olsen."

"Kathy, you are an angel. What do I owe you?" Adam asked after slowly resuming an upright, seated position.

"One thing. Just one thing. Just tell me what the hell happened. It's okay. Bradly's family."

Adam hesitated. He wasn't sure what he wanted to do about his run-in with the Hudson boys, but after all the help Kathy had given him, he felt an explanation was necessary. He told Kathy and Bradly the story about the Hudson boys and their cattle-guard ambush.

"Damned, Pikers," she said. She looked at Bradly and repeated herself. "Damned, Pikers!"

"Goin' to arrest em?" Bradly asked.

"I don't have the authority."

"Goin' to turn 'em in?"

"I haven't decided," Adam said.

Kathy was on the phone to Doc Olsen almost before Adam could answer. She explained the situation without mentioning the Hudson brothers. "Good," she said, "And thank you. Brad and Mr. Thompson will be over in a few minutes."

"You okay to drive, Mr. Thompson?"

"Please, call me Adam. And, yes, I can drive."

"Bradly, why don't you ride along with him, so he'll know how to find Doc Olsen's office. He'll have to come back this way anyway on his way home."

"You bet," Brad answered. "Your truck okay to drive?"

"Seemed to be. The rearview mirror is dangling, but nothing else seemed wrong. Guess a little ride would let me check it out."

On the way out the door, he felt a little dizzy. He said, "You know the way. Do you mind driving, Brad?"

"Not at all. I'll bet you're kinda tired."

"Yes, indeed," Adam said.

2

Stitches

Doc Olsen was an old country doctor—wizened and pleasant. His office was in his home, which was also worn around the edges, but welcoming. He met Adam and Brad at the door. He took a quick look at Adam and directed him to his examination room and invited Brad to make himself comfortable in the living room.

"There's coffee in the kitchen, Brad," he said. "Please help yourself. This may take a minute or two."

Doc Olsen followed Adam into the exam room and closed the door. The room was a vintage 1960s exam room. There was a small refrigerator, a countertop with multiple drawers underneath, a scale, and a wheeled stool, which had worn a discolored path on the linoleum floor surrounding the examination table. Obligatory diplomas and licenses adorned the walls right alongside a framed print of Norman Rockwell's painting of a small boy in a doctor's office about to get a shot in his rump.

Doc didn't spend time with introductions, insurance cards, or health history forms. He went right to work.

"Now, let me see that cut. Please lie back on that table." He removed Kathy's bandage and positioned an overhead light to illuminate the wound. "Oh, I see. Yep, those boys got you good, didn't they?"

It was evident the doctor had been briefed on his injury. News traveled fast in this part of Frederick County. "Well, I'll say this. My head was no match for my rearview mirror."

"I'm going to give you a nice little four-stitch tuck. Now, the edges of the wound are a little rough. I'll trim them up some so the scar will be less noticeable. There'll be a scar, but it won't scare people. Means I need to deaden you up a little bit. You allergic to anything?"

"Nope."

"How about the Hudsons?" Doc said with a smile.

"Yeah, I guess those guys make me itch a little. You got anything I can take for that?" Adam asked.

"I wish there was. Indeed, I do. Hold your head still now. This will sting a little." Doc Olsen slipped a needle into the swollen skin on Adam's forehead. Adam kept his eyes open and watched Doc's thumb press the syringe plunger. Numbness soon overtook the throbbing pain. Lying down felt good, and he started to drift off.

"This won't take long, Mr. Thompson. You'll feel a tug or two, but that's about all. Are you ready?" Doc asked.

"Do your thing, Doc," was Adam's foggy answer.

The entire procedure didn't take more than ten minutes. Doc switched off the examination light and repositioned it away from the table. "You can rest here for a while if you like. I'll be back in a moment." He left the room.

Adam was bone tired but determined to start home and be as far away from Snyder as possible. However, he lost his battle with fatigue and fell asleep. Fifteen minutes later, Doc Olsen was at his side gently nudging his shoulder.

"Mr. Thompson, I hate to wake you, but there's someone in the living room who would like to meet you. Do you feel well enough to do that?"

"Sure, I guess. Sorry, I didn't mean to doze off on you. Someone wants to meet me?"

Doc opened the door and let Adam enter the living room first. There, seated on the couch, sat Bradly and a khaki-shirted deputy sheriff. Both men stood as Adam entered the room. The deputy's badge and shoes were magnificently shined. He was young, eager, and regrettably transparent. The deputy adjusted his gun belt, wedging his right thumb behind the belt so that his right hand dangled in front of his holster. It was apparent to Adam the deputy enjoyed his job a little too much.

Brad spoke first. "Adam, this here's Deputy Hargrove. He heard about your trouble with the Hudsons, and he wants to help you."

Deputy Hargrove walked across the worn Persian rug and extended his hand. "Nice to meet you, Mr. Thompson. Hope you feel like talking a little."

Adam shook Hargrove's hand and said, "Sure. What's on your mind, Deputy? Mind if I sit?" He crossed the room and sat in a swivel chair, which faced the couch. He didn't want to be the middleman on a three-person couch ever again. Doc Olsen pulled up a straight-backed chair and flanked the sofa on the other side.

"Could you tell me what happened?" Hargrove said. "Kathy gave me her version, but I'd sure like to hear yours. If what she said is true, I'll bet we can take some action against those boys that'll give you a little satisfaction."

Adam was wide awake now. "You know, Deputy . . . was it Hargrave?

"Hargrove," he corrected.

"Well, Deputy Hargrove, I really don't know what I want to do."

"I just assumed you'd want to press charges," explained Deputy Hargrove.

"What would those charges be, do you suppose?"

"Tell me your story so I can give you some options."

Adam hadn't had time to think much, but he had a bad feeling about having any further contact with the Hudsons. "I'll tell you what happened, but don't consider it an agreement to press charges. I'm not sure my employer would want the publicity. And I am fairly sure that I have better things to do with my time." He told a condensed version of the story, emphasizing his sudden and dangerous meeting with the open ditch. He was surprised at how his anger escalated as he told the story, but he was careful to keep it suppressed.

"Sounds like at least reckless endangerment to me," Deputy Hargrove said. "Maybe worse. It was an on-purpose act. I'll bet we could make an aggravated battery charge stick. That would probably mean jail time. I can't think of a better use of your time than that."

"Do I have to decide now?"

"Sooner the better. If we write it up today, I can get up there in the morning and get a picture of the cattle-guard trap. Plus, we'd love to have a picture of your banged-up eyebrow while it still looks a little rugged. I've got a camera in the car."

"I want to slow down a little," Adam said. "Why don't we do this? You go ahead and take your picture. I'll take the time to talk to my boss and let you know what we decide as soon as I can tomorrow."

"Sit tight. I'll get my camera," Deputy Hargrove said. He rushed out the door to his squad car.

Brad spoke up. "You'd sure be doing us a big favor if you decide to press charges."

"What?" Adam asked.

"We all hate the Hudson brothers."

"Maybe I can explain," Doc Olsen interrupted. "The Hudsons are shameless bullies. They have tormented the people around here for as long as anyone can remember."

Deputy Hargrove returned with his camera. "Okay, Mr. Thompson. Please move over by the window so I can take a shot of your cut. It won't take a minute."

"You need light?" Doc said. "Come on into the exam room, and we'll do this right." All three men crowded into the small room. Adam eased up onto the exam table. Doc turned on the examination light, aimed it at the wound, and carefully removed the bandage. Deputy Hargrove hovered, focused, and took the photo.

"Good work, Deputy," Doc Olsen said. "Now, please move into the living room so I can redo his bandage and get Mr. Thompson on his way. The deputy left, and Doc Olsen returned his attention to Adam.

"We could've taken the picture in the living room, but I wanted a private word with you," Doc said, as he gathered his scissors, tape, and gauze to renew Adam's bandage. "I think it's important for you to understand what you'd be up against if you press charges. The Hudsons are criminals. They fight hard and usually win. They have a sleazy attorney out of Omaha who usually finds a loophole to get them off. That's why people put up with them. They think trying to beat them legally is a waste of time."

"What sort of things do they do?" Adam asked.

Doc cut the gauze into a precise two-inch square, as he talked. "The list is long. They've slashed tires. They've stolen unbranded cattle. They've poisoned wells. Folks think they're the ones who shot holes in the water tower. They've been banned from the Snyder tavern because they sliced the pool table felt the full length of the table just for the fun of it. And, that's just the stuff we know about. Of course, there's never enough evidence or witnesses willing testify to convict them."

"Why are they so difficult to get along with? Do you have any idea?" Adam asked.

"Sometimes when people, start down a path it's hard to change directions," Doc said, as he cut the adhesive tape into two perfectly sized strips. "The Hudsons are hardscrabble family. They've been on that farm for three generations. From what I hear, they've always lived with one foot outside the law and one insult away from a feud with their neighbors."

"You sound like you know them well."

"I've lived here all my life. I've always been interested in the history and the ebb and flow of the community. The Hudsons, despite their contrariness, are certainly a colorful part of it. Besides, in my business, it pays to know who'll pay ya and who won't. Doc carefully repositioned Adam's head so he had easy access to Adam's wound. "Now, lie still while I finish this up."

With his fresh bandage in place, Adam sat up on the examination table and dangled his legs over the edge. "One foot outside the law? You make it sound almost forgivable."

"Some of it is. Some of it isn't," Doc said, as he repositioned his stool so his patient wouldn't have to turn his aching head. "Grandpa Jedidiah Hudson was quick to see the silver lining of Prohibition. They made bootleg whiskey. Whiskey profits are what allowed them to prosper during the Great Depression when so many others fell on hard times. That's when Grandfather Jedidiah expanded his agricultural ambitions. He bought additional land adjacent to the original farm and built the house they live in today. Back then, some folks thought they'd turned a corner and would finally be able to settle in as good citizens."

"Nobody blamed them much for being bootleggers?" Adam asked.

"Everybody had to find a way to get by in those days, and everybody hated Prohibition anyway. The trouble was old habits die hard. The Hudsons found a new source of illicit revenue during World War II. They sold black market tires. Tires were in short supply. They were one of the first things to be rationed and they stayed that way for the duration of the war. People couldn't find tires anywhere. And there sat the Hudson's with tires galore. Using their bootlegging connections, they stockpiled a barn full of them, which they sold at prices sometimes five times the prewar cost."

"Resourceful, weren't they? Not very patriotic, but resourceful."

"Oh, yes, always resourceful. During Prohibition, if you wanted a drink, you talked to the Hudsons. During the war years, if you wanted tires, you talked to the Hudsons. After the war, nobody talked to the Hudsons. They were shunned, even by those who had secretly bought their black market tires."

"That must've stung a little."

"Yep. Their inbred defensiveness became meanness. Forty years later, being contrary is not a choice for Rufus, Harley, and Ricky. It's inherited. They probably know little about bootleg whiskey and black market tires. All they know is people in these parts hate 'em, and they hate people right back. It's the reason for their meanness and, at times, outright hostility. Rufus, in particular, is a nasty one.

"Well, it's nice to know all that, Doc, but it doesn't make my head feel any better."

"Then you, your wounded forehead, and out-of-town innocence come along. All that combined with an official government job, and people see you as the perfect way to even the score. And with you doing the dirty work, they don't have to worry about personal reprisals if the charges don't stick. Now, I am not telling you what to do. I'd love to see those boys get thumped, but I just wanted you to know the Hudson brothers are not just three overzealous farm boys having a good time. They are dangerous troublemakers. They know how to fight."

Adam said nothing. He frowned and shook his head.

"I think you're good to go," Doc Olsen said. "Good luck, Mr. Thompson. Good luck."

"Thank you, Doc. What do I owe you?" Adam asked, reaching for his wallet.

"Fifteen bucks," Doc said. Adam paid him. Doc was just behind Adam with his hand on his left shoulder as they walked into the living room.

"Well, there you are and as good as new," Deputy Hargrove said.

"Deputy, I will call you tomorrow. Right now, I need to get Bradly home and be on my way," Adam said, unwilling to talk further.

"That'll be fine. I think you've got a case here, but what you do is up to you. The real reason I came here was to make sure you didn't circle back up there and try to take care of things on your own. I was seriously afraid you might blow up their house or something,"

"You were afraid, were you?" Adam spoke without a smile. "Fear is a wish, Deputy. Fear is a wish."

"What?" the deputy asked.

"Never mind. Bradly, let's get going."

3

Unfamiliar Dread

AFTER DROPPING BRAD OFF at the antique store, Adam pulled into the Shell station for gas and to call home. He told Connie only that he was going to be a little late because one of his stops took a little longer than usual. There would be plenty of time for her to worry. No need for her to begin now.

The ride home was slow but welcome. The pickup's shimmy kept him from driving over fifty miles per hour. Still, escaping the incessant counsel of the village grocer, the antique merchant, the spit-shined deputy, and the country doctor was a relief. Although his head still hurt, his mind was unusually clear. He wanted to share his story with his own people before deciding what to do, which would include his family and his boss, Hubert St. John, the county commissioner of Frederick County.

Connie was first. When he pulled in the driveway, it was nearly dark, and the kitchen light was on. He entered through the back door, which led directly to the kitchen. She was at the table, clipping coupons. Adam let the door slam, dropped his bag, and entered the room with a broad smile on his face. She saw the bandage above his right eye, saw the smile, and said, "Adam, what in the world!"

He walked to the refrigerator, grabbed a cold soda, and joined Connie at the table. "First of all, I'm okay. It looks worse than it is. But I've had quite a day." He told her what happened, although he didn't elaborate on the communal hatred for the Hudson brothers he had discovered.

"Let me take you to the emergency room," she said.

"No, I think my friendly country doctor in Elwood did a good job. Right now, I need to call St. John to tell him what happened. Then I am off to bed. I am dog tired."

He placed his chair beneath the wall phone mounted at the end of the kitchen counter. County Commissioner Hubert St. John was watching *The Cosby Show* on television when he received the call. They knew each other well.

"Hubert, this is Adam. I'm sorry to bother you at home, but I had some difficulty during my trip north to Snyder today. Let me give you the short version, and maybe we can meet tomorrow sometime to discuss it further."

"Difficulty?" Hubert replied.

"Yes, I had a minor car accident. I cut my head bad enough to need stitches. I'm home, and I'm okay. The pickup will need minor repair. It's the circumstances that led to the accident that will be of greater concern to our department, I think." He gave Hubert an abbreviated explanation of the cattle guard incident, the local deputy's involvement, and the community's prevailing opinion about the Hudson brothers. "My question is simple. Do we press charges or not? I hope we can talk more about it all tomorrow. I'm pretty tired right now."

"You bet we can. Are you sure you're okay? You've seen a doctor, right?"

"I have. I'm already stitched up. Country doc up in Elwood did it."

"Good. I think I can rearrange my day without a problem. Let's tentatively plan to meet at ten in the morning. If that must change, I'll call you back. I'm so sorry you're hurt, Adam, and don't worry about a thing. Just get some rest, and I'll see you in the morning."

After he hung up the phone, Adam couldn't take one step further than his overstuffed recliner in the living room. He sat, laid back, and said, "Connie, would you call the boys." In seconds he was fast asleep.

Connie listened carefully to her husband's end of the conversation, hoping to learn more about what happened. The only new thing she learned was that the Hudson brothers were not popular people.

Thirty minutes later the phone rang. "Hello, Ms. Thompson, is Adam available? This is Hubert St. John."

"Well, he's here, but he's sleeping, and I hate to wake him." Connie responded. Can I give him a message?

"Sure, but first, how is he? Did he seem pretty banged up? If I know Adam, he'd probably downplay the seriousness of is injury."

"I haven't seen beneath the bandage yet, but it's a big one, and his eye is starting to get black. I just haven't seen him so tired in a long time." Connie felt the need to check on Adam but couldn't because she was tethered to the wall phone by its short cord.

"Sounds like he had quite an ordeal up there. I need to know more, but I'm sure Adam handled things perfectly. Listen, I called to reschedule our meeting. Tell him I've invited the county attorney to join us, and he isn't free until one o'clock tomorrow. Would you ask him to meet us in my office then?"

"County attorney?" Connie questioned.

"Oh, it's no big deal, but it sounded like some legal advice may be necessary, and I just wanted to get everything done at one time if we can. I'm sure Adam would agree with that."

"I see. Yes, I will sure tell him."

"Great. Thank you. And tell Adam if he's not feeling well enough to meet tomorrow, we can easily reschedule. Goodbye."

"I will tell him. Thanks for your concern, Hubert. I guess this is one we'll just have to play by ear. Goodbye."

Connie took a deep breath and went into the living room to check on her husband. Her concern transcended his wounded eyebrow. How it was wounded was equally troubling. During their forty-year marriage she'd nursed him through dozens of accidental cuts and bruises, a severely sprained ankle, and a dislocated shoulder. This wound was different and came with unfamiliar dread. It was not unintended. It was the first to be purposely inflicted by another person, and Adam's easy-going ways didn't protect him. She kissed the left side of his forehead, removed his shoes, covered him with an afghan, and returned to the kitchen to call Mike and Scott.

~~~~~~~

Mike was the older of the Adam and Connie's two sons. He owned a welding shop in Spring Valley and thought he knew every farmer in the county. He was surprised he didn't know the Hudsons. He walked in the back door at his parent's house at eight o'clock the next morning. "How's Dad doing? Is he up?"

"He's movin' around up there. I think he smelled the coffee. I let him sleep in his chair until about midnight, then I helped him upstairs. I want to get him in to see Dr. Jacobson just to double-check what that country doctor did to him," Mom said.

"Did he tell you any more about what happened?" Mike asked as he took a seat at the kitchen table. His mother poured him coffee.

"Nope. I've told you all I know."

They heard his street-shoed footsteps as he came down the stairs. Mike half expected to see him wearing a bathrobe and slippers. Instead, he was shaved and dressed for work, even though Connie told him he didn't need to meet with Hubert St. John until that afternoon. He grinned when he saw Mike.

"Morning, Dad," Mike said.

"Morning, Mike. Thanks for coming over."

Connie placed a cup of hot coffee on the table in front of his chair and touched the chair back with three easy pats, inviting her husband to sit. "I'd like you to see Doc Jacobson today. What do you think?"

"Doubt if I can get in today, but I should see him. Like to have him take a look at these stitches. Doc in Elwood said they'd dissolve in ten days or so. Still, be a good idea to have Doc Jacobson take a look. Yeah, call him, would you, Connie?" He returned his attention to Mike. "Mom tell you what happened?"

"She did, but I'd like to hear your version. I'll bet she'd like to hear it again too. It's such an unlikely story. We don't want to miss a thing."

He had told the complete story twice the day before. Both those tellings were throbbing renditions offered closer to the heat of the moment. This would be the first time he could tell it slowly with nuanced, reflective detail to two people he loved. Twenty minutes and two cups of coffee later, he stopped talking.

"Hudson brothers? Like I said, never heard of them. I'll bet Norm Benton knows them. He sells tractors all over the county." Norm Benton owned a John Deere dealership in Spring Valley. "Not important, I guess. What's important is you. Man, oh, man, I'm glad your home, Dad."

"Me too," Connie said, as she walked to the wall phone to call Dr. Jacobson.

"Me too." Adam said with a smile.

"Did you call Scott?" Mike asked. "He and Sally need to know."

"Yes. He was as shocked as we were. He said they'd come home this weekend to see Dad." Younger brother Scott and his wife, Sally, were college professors at a small college in Chanute, Nebraska. They made the two-hour drive home to Spring Valley often.

"Please don't make a mountain out of a molehill, guys" Adam said. "I'm okay. I'm just fine. There's no need to worry everybody. I know how it happened is probably a good story, but the story is one thing. The bump on my head is another. I am okay."

"We will worry if we want too," Connie said.

"I know you will, Connie. I know you will. And I appreciate it."

"What's next?" Mike asked.

"I don't know. I'll know more after I talk with St. John this afternoon. I think it's best not to talk to anyone about it until I do. Mike, would you call Scott and tell him to keep it under his hat?"

"I will," Mike said. He reached across the table and placed his hand on his dad's arm. "Thanks for filling me in, Dad. Glad you're okay. I'm taking off now. I'll check in with you tonight. Go slow today. Okay?"

Mike would have called Scott even if his father hadn't him asked. From a distance, Mike and Scott were as different as night and day. Close up, they were an inseparable team whose unembarrassed love for one another was immeasurable. Mike was street smart and immediate. Scott was thoughtful and ponderous. Their affection for one another started with an appreciation for those differences.

The first thing Mike did after he got to the shop was call Scott. "Hey, Scott. Mom called you about Dad last night, right?"

"She did. I was about to call you. What an unbelievable story. What do you make of it, and how is Dad?"

"He seems fine. I was over there first thing this morning. He seemed fine. Big bandage and a black eye, but up and at 'em."

"Tell me what you know. Mom was tired and hurried last night when she called. I wasn't sure I heard what I heard. Tell me what you know."

Mike carefully repeated the surprising story of his dad's cattle-guard ambush. "After all that, he only has four stitches and a pickup with alignment issues," Mike concluded. "And he's meeting with his boss and the county attorney this afternoon to decide what to do next."

"County attorney? Is he going to press charges?" Scott asked.

"I don't know. My guess is, if it were up to Dad, he'd leave it alone and let the Hudson brothers be eaten alive by their noxious weeds. But, since he was on the job and the pickup is government property, it may not be up to him.

"I told Mom that we'd be home this Saturday. If there are any new developments, please let me know. Otherwise, I'll see you on Saturday."

"One more thing. Dad asked that we not talk to anyone about this until he knows more about next steps. Okay?"

"Sure. Of course, Sally already knows. It is one hell of a story to tell though, isn't it? If you learn anything new, call me. Thanks for calling, Mike. I'm off to class. Goodbye."

"Goodbye. See you Saturday," Mike said.

Scott picked up his backpack and was out the door. He was anxious to share what he'd learned about Adam's condition and the meeting with the county attorney with Sally. She had early classes, so she was already on campus. She and her father-in-law adored one another.

Adam and Sally began teasing each other on the first day they met over two years before. She and Scott were not yet married, and she endeared herself to the whole family with her playful ways—especially Adam. Adam had just accepted his job as weed supervisor. While they were having dinner, he began to expound on what he already knew about weeds and the damage they could cause. He stopped when he realized he was focusing too much on himself in the presence of his first-time guest. He abruptly changed the subject. "So, Sally, you are from North Carolina, right? How do you like Nebraska?"

"Oh, I love it," she answered. "But there is one thing that has always concerned me."

"What's that?" Adam asked.

"There are too darned many weeds."

Everyone laughed, especially Adam.

4

The Barn

HUBERT ST. JOHN ROSE from behind his grey metal desk when he saw Adam approaching his office, which was on the second floor of the Frederick County Courthouse. He met Adam at the door, placing one hand on Adam's shoulder and the other on his forearm. He physically guided Adam to one of two chairs in front of his desk.

No, need for all that, Hubert," Adam said. "I'm no worse for the wear. A little uglier, but I'm okay." The afternoon sun brightened the unadorned room through tall, bare windows behind Hubert's desk. Adam held his three-ring binder tight against his chest and scooted his chair slightly to avoid the glare. He had replaced Doc Olsen's bright-white gauze dressing with a skin-toned, store-bought bandage, which was only slightly less noticeable. There was no easy way to camouflage his black eye.

"What a day you had, my friend. What a day!" Hubert said as he circled the desk and sat. "Doc up in Elwood patch you up okay, did he?"

"I think so. His name's Olsen. His stitch work looks okay to me. Still, Connie wants me to see Dr. Jacobson just to be sure everything is good. I'll do that after we finish here. He was able to sneak me in. He'll just take a look and turn me loose, I expect.

"Interesting thing was how much Doc Olsen knew about the Hudson brothers. In addition to patching my eye, he helped me understand who we're dealing with," Adam said.

"Hold that thought until Salisbury gets here."

County Commissioner Hubert St. John was a stout, stylish little man. He wore red suspenders over his white dress shirt and a red and yellow paisley bow tie. Suspenders and bow ties were his trademark. Why he needed a signature look puzzled many people, and many of them thought he was a wannabe bigwig. Adam knew better. When a coworker made a snide remark about Hubert's fancy, "go-to-hell" bow tie, he didn't mince words. "He is a good man," Adam said. "He treats me with absolute respect and, believe me, he knows what he's doing. I don't much care if he wears his pajamas to work."

"How'd you get here? I suppose you left your truck at the Ford garage, didn't you?" Hubert asked.

"Yes, first thing. Connie followed me over. I took her home and drove over here in her car. Thanks for telling the Ford guys I was coming."

"Do you know Jason Salisbury, the county attorney? He's running a little late, but he's eager to hear your story. I told him as much as I knew, but I'm sure you can fill in some blanks for us. This doesn't mean that we're going to go to war with the Hudsons, but Jason must learn about it at some point, and I thought it would be good to get it all done in one sitting. Are you tired of telling your story?"

"Not at all, but I'm getting rather good at it. And I wish it was just a story. Of course, I know who Jason is, but I've never met him," Adam said.

Jason reached inside the room and knocked on the frosted window of the open door. His crisp buttoned-down shirt, striped tie, and cordovan wingtips said lawyer before he opened his mouth. "Gentlemen, is this the Hudson brothers summit?" Jason asked. Then he looked across the room at Adam and his wounded forehead and thought better of his attempt at humor. "Hello, I'm Jason Salisbury. You must be Adam Thompson. It's nice to meet you, and I'm sorry about your run-in with our neighbors to the north." He crossed the room, motioning for Adam to remain seated, shook

Adam's hand, and sat in the empty chair. He was about thirty-five years old, tanned and fit, and had an inviting, believable smile.

"Thanks for coming, Jason," Hubert said. "I'm glad you were able to make it over to hear the story directly. You ready?" Hubert was anxious to hear the story again.

"I am. Yes, I am. But, first, how are you doing, Adam?"

"I'll survive," Adam said.

"Before you begin, I have a couple of questions for you, Adam." Jason said. "Hubert gave me a snapshot of what happened to you. I just want to know a little more about what's normal for you. Does anyone ever resist your request to kill noxious weeds?"

"Seldom, if ever. I've had people question my authority a couple of times. But it's always been just a little hot air rather than serious resistance. They usually do what's asked of them. In two years, I've had very few people who needed a little nudge after the initial citation."

"How about the Hudsons? Did you give them a citation?"

"Yes, I did," Adam said. He opened his binder, removed the citation from the side pocket, and handed the document, complete with his bloody thumbprint, to Salisbury.

"Whoa. Is that blood?"

"Yes."

"Yours, I presume."

"Yes. At first, I decided that writing them up during my first visit would be unwise. I simply told them that I'd be back to check on their progress in a couple of weeks. Then I hit their ditch and changed my mind. I completed the citation and put it in their mailbox and drove back to Snyder."

"Why did you initially decide not to give them a citation?" Jason asked.

"I think you'll understand, once you hear my story,"

"Okay. Just one more question. Did you see or notice anything odd or out of the ordinary while you were there? We have other reasons to be interested in the Hudsons."

"The entire stop in Snyder was odd, from start to finish," Adam said.

"Okay, Adam. Your turn. I won't interrupt again."

Jason scribbled notes as Adam talked. Adam started with the unexpected warning from Kathy, the grocer, and ended with Doc Olsen's assessment of the Hudson brothers. He even mentioned the oozy-eyed cat and the curious words in the dust on his back window. He added that he was unsure about how to respond to Deputy Hargrove's eagerness to prosecute.

Jason stopped writing and looked up from his notepad. "What did you just say?" he asked.

"I said Deputy Hargrove was eager to prosecute."

"No, before that. You said there was a message written in the dust on your back window. What was it, again?"

"It was just two words: The Barn. That's all it said. Just 'The Barn.' Looked like it was written in a hurry. Is it important?"

"It could be," Jason said. Then he paused, clicked his ballpoint pen twice, and said, "What I am about to tell you is not to be shared with anyone. Not anyone. Got it?" He shifted in his chair twice, so that he could address each man separately.

"Hubert?"

"Certainly," answered Hubert.

"Adam?"

"Of course."

"As you may know, a ten-year-old boy is missing. His name is Jimmy Tedrow, and he's been missing for two days. This morning Sheriff Bartlow received a cryptic phone call. All the caller said was, 'Rufus has him.' Then he hung up. We are still unsure what to make of it. There are four people named Rufus who live in Frederick County, including Snyder's Rufus Hudson. You may have just narrowed the field."

"Wait a minute, Jason," Adam said. "This could be nothing, but you asked if I'd seen anything odd or out of place. There was a bike. The only reason I noticed it was because it was one of the only signs of life around the house. Other than the bike and the fresh gravel on the driveway, the place looked abandoned. It was a kid's red bicycle. It was shoved behind one of the overgrown bushes alongside the house. Odd place for a kid's bike, don't you think?"

"Yes, I do," Jason answered. "Three bachelors wouldn't need a kid's bike." He paused and shifted gears. He talked fast. "This feels like progress. I'm unsure if a missing bike is part of Jimmy's story, but I'll find out. There's still a lot that doesn't make sense. We know Rufus Hudson isn't a very pleasant person, but kidnapping a kid from his hometown is crazy. And why in God's name would he mess with you when he's holding a kidnapped boy in his barn? Did he seem stupid or crazy when you talked to him?"

"Oh, he's not stupid. But, he's volatile, I'll tell you that. Mad as hell one second and relatively pleasant the next. Crazy? I don't know about that. Thinking back, seems like my ditch dive was little more than spur-of-the-moment entertainment for them. Could be a government guy in a government pickup was just too much to pass up."

"Entertainment? Jason asked, as he placed his notepad on the edge of Hubert's desk, stood, and circled slowly behind Adam's chair. "Suppose they simply wanted, or needed, to take their minds off the boy in the barn for a moment. Adam, maybe you were a welcomed diversion for them."

"That wouldn't surprise me. Nothing you could say about the Hudson brothers would surprise me."

"Well, if that's true, their need for diversionary amusement may have done them in." Jason clicked his pen twice and returned to his chair. "Adam, are there any other farms near the Hudson place?"

"It's four miles north of Snyder and it's the only farm until you get to Pike County, which is another three miles north."

"Does the farmhouse sit close to the road?"

"No. Their house sits well off the road. Probably a couple hundred yards."

"So, there's not much chance that someone saw something and reported it? There are no close neighbors to see anything and a passerby sighting of anything suspicious is unlikely. Is that a fair assessment?"

"Yes. I'd say that sizes it up pretty well," Adam answered.

Salisbury raced toward an unproven conclusion that he wanted to chase further. "There are other options. At first, we thought it might have been a prank call. You know, somebody trying to set Rufus up just to mess with him. But the bike, the phone call, and your dusty message suggest otherwise. It looks like someone, maybe one of the brothers, believes kidnapping crosses the line. I understand, they've done a lot of detestable things, but never something this serious. So, you were with two of the brothers inside the house, right? Rufus and Harley, right?"

"That's right."

"You never saw the third brother while you were in the house, did you? What's his name?"

"It's Ricky. And you're right. I saw all three of them celebrating on the front porch after I hit the ditch, but while I was at the house, I didn't see Ricky. You think he's the guy who wrote on my window and made the call?"

"It makes sense, doesn't it? He was outside on the tractor, right? He had easy access to your pickup's back window. And you're sure the message wasn't there before you got to the Hudson's?"

"I would have noticed. Besides, the truck wasn't dusty until I drove up their lane."

What do you know about the brothers as individuals? Anything?"

"Nothing, absolutely nothing."

"By tomorrow, I should know more. But right now, for Jimmy's sake, I need to talk to a judge. Adam, you don't mind if we put your complaint on hold for a couple of days, do you?"

"My head will heal. Find the child," Adam answered.

"Excuse me, gentlemen. I'll keep you both in the loop, but, please, say nothing to anybody about this. Not your wife. Not your kids. Not your preacher or your bartender. I'll talk to you soon. And don't go too far away. We may need you." Salisbury double-timed his wingtips out the door and down the marble-floored corridor of the Fredrick County Courthouse.

Adam and Hubert sat quietly for a moment looking at one another. Hubert finally spoke. "Well, when I woke up this morning, I never dreamed I'd be knee-deep in a kidnapping case. How about you?"

"Never in a thousand years, Hubert."

"It appears your bumpy trip to Snyder may have a silver lining."

"Maybe so. Maybe so. If they find the boy, I'll wear my stitches proudly?"

"Listen, there may be something more we can do to help. You have a camera in your pickup, don't you?"

"Yes, sir. I'm an excellent noxious-weed photographer." Adam smiled when he said it.

"Run over to the Ford garage. See if there is anything left of the dusty message on your back window. If there is, get a picture of it. It could come in handy. I'd go with you, but I want to stay here in case Salisbury calls."

When Adam got to the garage, his pickup was untouched. It sat next to be serviced in a short line of cars at the mechanics' bay door, and the afternoon sun hit the back window at a revealing angle. The thickest dust was gone, but a light, gritty film remained. It held the finger-written lettering with enough contrast that "The Barn" was clearly legible. He took the shot from several angles, which gave him another idea. Maybe there was a fingerprint within the dusty note. He used the garage phone to called Hubert.

"Hubert, this is Adam. Good news. The words are still legible. I've taken several shots, but what about fingerprints? Do you think we should have someone come take a look?"

"Great idea," Hubert said. "I'll call Jason. Where's the truck now? Is it inside?"

"No, it's outside, next in line to be worked on."

"Tell them not to work on it, but to pull it inside if possible. We'll postpone the work until tomorrow. For now, there've been some developments you should know about."

"What's up?" Adam asked.

"Two state patrolmen and the county sheriff are on their way to Snyder as we speak." Hubert said. "They'll team up with your Deputy Hargrove and go straight to the Hudson place to search the barn, and the house too, if necessary. Salisbury was able to get a warrant based on what you told him. Seems Jimmy's bike went missing with him. The bike, the note on your window, plus the suspicious phone call sealed the deal. All we do now is wait."

"Been an interesting couple of days," Adam said. "And it looks like we might have a couple more."

"I'm afraid you're right. Now, go see your doctor."

"Don't keep me in the dark over the weekend. If something happens, please call me."

"I'll keep you posted," Hubert said.

5
—

Unrevealed

SALLY AND SCOTT ARRIVED at Adam and Connie's house a little before ten o'clock on Saturday morning. Adam was napping in his recliner as they entered the living room through the front door. A fishing program was on television, the volume low. Connie peeked in from the kitchen, smiled, put her finger to her lips, motioning for them to join her. They placed their overnight bags by the front door and tiptoed past sleeping Adam into the kitchen and toward a pot of hot coffee.

"How is he doing?" Sally asked, as she took Connie's hands in her own. "And how are you doing?"

"Oh, we're fine. Adam's a little beat up, but he'll be okay. He doesn't look fine. He's got a plum-colored shiner and a few stitches above his eyebrow, but Doc Jacobson checked him out yesterday and said the healing process is right on track. He said the country doctor who patched him up did a great job.

"You guys sit down and have a cup of coffee. How about a brownie? Molly brought them over yesterday."

"Mike told us what happened. But his story only went as far as it went. I mean, what's new with this situation? Is Dad going to press charges?" Scott asked.

"It's not a simple answer. I'll let your Dad tell you about that."

Adam yelled from the living room, "Who you talking to, Connie?"

"It's Scott and Sally. They just got here."

With that, Sally got up, ran to the living room, and knelt beside Adam's recliner almost before Scott could swallow his first sip of coffee.

"Hey, Dad. How're you feeling?"

"I'm okay. Just enjoying my chair. That's all."

Sally reached up and gently touched his chin, turning his head so she could get a better look at the damage. "Wow! That's a pretty one. You do things right, don't you?'

"I had some help on this one."

"That's what we heard," Sally said. "Feel like talking about it, or would you rather rest?"

"I thought I heard someone talking about brownies. Bring me one, and I'll tell you all about it," He winked with his left eye when he said it.

Scott placed the brownie, a cup of coffee, and a goofy get-well card on the tray table beside Adam's chair. Sally turned off the TV, and Adam started talking and didn't stop until he had taken them to the Hudson's place and back to Spring Valley.

"That's incredible," Scott said. "I hope your nail them to the wall, Dad. Have you pressed charges?"

"Not yet. And for good reason, but it's a reason that I can't share with you yet. You're going to have to be patient with me on this one."

"He won't even tell me," Connie complained.

"Look. All I can say is, and I shouldn't even say this, if you were surprised by the first chapter, you'll be staggered by the second. Now, don't quiz me about this like a bunch of Pikers."

"Like a bunch of what?" Sally asked.

"Pikers," he answered. Then he slowly explained its meaning. He told them how he had learned the word and how commonplace it was in Snyder. It was apparent he didn't want to return to questions about the mysterious second chapter, so they didn't.

The phone rang. Connie ran to answer it. Adam stirred and brought the recliner's footrest down, suspecting the call would be for him.

"It's for you, Adam," Connie said. "You want me to take a message?"

Adam's answer was abrupt and forceful. "No. I'll take it. You guys stay put." Then he smiled and offered a playful excuse for his sharp response. "I don't want you to hear my foul language." He went to the kitchen and took the phone, directing Connie back to the living room with a couple of quick flicks of his wrist. His need for privacy increased everyone's curiosity.

As he expected, the call was from Hubert. "Adam, how are you feeling this morning?

"Not bad. Not bad at all. Amazing what a little sleep will do for you. What's up?"

"I have good news and bad news," Hubert said. "The good news is we think we're right about the Hudsons having Jimmy. The sheriff found evidence of someone having slept in the hayloft, chained to a beam. The bad news is, there was no boy, no bike, and not a Hudson brother to be found. The sheriff and his men searched the barn and the house, and another broken-down outbuilding, which appeared to be an old chicken coop. They found nothing. Darkness stopped them from searching the hilly pasture behind the house. They will return today to do that, but I don't hold much hope for that search.

"I wonder how they knew we were on to them?"

"Nobody knows. Maybe they felt vulnerable at their farm because of the way they treated you. Maybe the enormity of their crime finally sank in. For whatever reason, they decided to lay low somewhere else. They hadn't been gone long though if the fresh milk in the refrigerator is any indication.

"Nuts," Adam said. "Were they able to check my window for fingerprints?"

"There was one retrievable print. Don't know who it belongs to though. Janson's betting on Ricky. Me too, I guess."

"How about my truck. Will they be able to work on it on Monday?"

"Yes, we'll get it in first thing Monday morning. Adam, we'll still nail them for the dirty trick they pulled on you, but that'll have to wait until we see how this Tedrow thing works out."

"That is the least of my worries, Hubert. If it's up to me, I say we drop it altogether. There's a ten-year-old boy missing. Pursuing them for my bumped head would be pole-vaulting over mouse turds, wouldn't it?"

"I suppose. I'll ask Jason what he thinks, but, as far as I'm concerned, it's up to you."

"Let's concentrate on Jimmy," Adam said. "What else can I do? Should I get a loaner vehicle and go to work tomorrow, or do you want me to sit tight for another day or two."

"Sit tight and heal, Adam. There's one more thing. Salisbury thinks it would be smart to continue to keep this under wraps, so please don't talk about it to anyone."

"Sure thing. Thanks for calling, Hubert. I'll check in with you Monday. You hear anything sooner, please let me know."

Adam walked back into the living room, shrugged his shoulders, and sat down. "Just St. John checking to see how I'm doing. He's a great guy to work for."

Everyone suspected he was hiding the truth. He had been on the phone too long for the call to be nothing more than a wellness check. No one forced the issue.

The Thompsons didn't go to church the next day because Adam didn't want to parade his wound around and have to answer a lot of questions. Instead, they went to Mike's house for brunch. After Adam entertained the group by fibbing to Mike's kids about what happened to his forehead, Scott cornered Mike on the back deck to see if he knew more. Mike was as puzzled as Scott. He did share what he'd learned about the Hudson brothers from his conversation with Norman Benton, the John Deere dealer in Spring Valley.

"I probably shouldn't have, but I told Norm Benton about what happened to Dad and asked if he knew the Hudson brothers. I thought he might have done business with them."

"Were you right?"

"Yep. He sold them a tractor a little over a year ago. Norm said all three of them came into his dealership at the same time. He claimed it was the strangest sale he'd ever made. The three brothers surrounded the tractor and attacked. They were on it, under it, over it, ogling it, and petting it. Norm didn't have to sell the tractor. They sold themselves. All three of them test-drove it, and all three of them crowded into Norm's office to close the deal. Norm said he looked across his desk at the three brothers, eager to see which one of them would sign the financing agreement. As it turned out, there was no agreement to sign. They paid him nearly twenty thousand dollars in cash."

"Unbelievable. One surprise after another," Scott said. "So, you know nothing about what's going to happen next? Dad was mum about it."

"When I asked, he simply showed me his palm. And you know Dad, he could keep a secret from God if he put his mind to it. I knew enough to let it alone. And you should too."

6

The Letter

DURING THEIR RIDE HOME, Sally and Scott spent the best part of two hours in wild speculation about Adam's secret. Did Dad do something more than just yell at the Hudsons after he hit the ditch? Did the Hudsons have skeletons in their closet that he accidentally uncovered? Maybe some of the weeds Dad found were more than noxious. Maybe they were illegal? Could marijuana have provided enough money to buy a tractor? Perhaps the deputy himself was profiting from the Hudson's criminal activity. Or the antique dealer. For goodness sake, who drives all the way to Snyder to buy antiques? Adam's entanglement in a kidnapping case never came to mind.

Tired of sitting, on Tuesday, he borrowed Connie's car and went to his office, which was in the basement of the courthouse. It was adequate but dungeonlike. He didn't mind because he spent so little time there. He walked in, turned on the flickering overhead fluorescent light, and grabbed his favorite coffee mug: a white mug adorned with dark-blue type, which read *Obnoxious Weed Supervisor*. It was a Christmas gift from Sally. He loved the cup just about as much as he loved playful Sally.

He had taken one step toward the hall and the community coffee pot when he glanced at his in-box. A curious, hand-addressed letter lay on top of the stack of routine paperwork. He circled the desk, put down the cup, picked up the envelope, examined it, and tore it open. The handwriting on the enclosed letter was irregular and unpracticed but written with determined neatness. He read it twice, picked up the phone, and called Hubert, who wasn't available. Then he called Jason Salisbury, who answered the phone himself.

"Jason, this is Adam Thompson. I've received a letter about the Tedrow case that you must read. Can I bring it up right now?"

"Of course, you can. Give me five minutes. I have someone with me, but Jimmy Tedrow is the most important thing on my docket."

Jason was alone at his massive wooden desk. Law books lined the walls of the room and a pull-down shade full of pinholes blocked most of the sun from entering the room. Adam walked in without knocking, handed the letter to Salisbury, and sat down in a cushioned side chair.

"You doing okay, Adam?" Jason asked as he took the letter.

"Feeling better all the time. Please, read."

The letter was addressed to Mr. Adam Thompson, noxious weed supervisor of Frederick County. It read as follows:

> *Dear Mr. Thompson,*
>
> *Rufus had your card so Im writin you. Sorry you hit the ditch so hard. Rufus said you looked like you was a man who could take a joke. Hope so. This heres why I'm writin. I got Jimmy Tedrow and I need help gettin him home. This heres the plan.*
>
> *Go to the blue bird diner in Elwood at 630 on friday morning. They open up then. Sit by the window. Ware a red cap and a blue shirt like you was warin at our place. Jimmy will be there by 7. Just you. Ain't you, no Jimmy. And no cops. Cops come, no Jimmy! He will already have ate. And drive your white pickup. Be sure to tell Keith Jimmy is ok.*
>
> *Ricky Hudson*

"Holy crap, Adam, When did you receive this?" Jason asked.

"I found it five minutes ago. Not sure when it landed on my desk. I wasn't here yesterday. It was postmarked last Saturday."

"This is all good news. At least we know they're still in the area. We'll keep the pressure on. Hopefully, we'll find him before

Friday. But, honestly, Adam, we don't have much else going. But this could work. We can have a deputy in a red hat and a blue shirt meet Jimmy, and they won't know the difference. We'll even put a bandage on his forehead."

Having a deputy take his place was not something Adam had considered. As he hurried from his basement office up the stairs to the second floor, he had already imagined himself waiting in the Bluebird Diner wearing a red cap. "I'm not so sure about that. Ricky wrote to me. They all know what I look like. They expect me. I should do it. Besides, it sounds like a safe enough plan. What can they do to me inside the cafe?"

"Are you sure?" Jason asked. "It would simplify our task." Jason paused, clicked his pen twice, and said, "Tell you what, I'll talk with Sheriff Bartlow. If he agrees, you're on."

"Seems to me like the surest way to get Jimmy Tedrow home," Adam said.

"You may be right, Adam. And, that is the task at hand. We will worry about the Hudson brothers later.

"Adam, we're damned lucky Ricky's letter came when it did. We were about to make a last-resort effort and go public with the Hudson brother's story in the hope that some citizen would lead us to them, but we don't have to do that now. No telling how an unstable mind will respond to that sort of pressure. This is the best news I've had all day. Have you told Hubert yet?

"No. I called, but he wasn't in. By the way, who is Keith? Do you know?"

"That's Jimmy's dad. There seems to be a high school connection somehow. Keith says he and Ricky were friendly but not close friends. Whatever it is, it seems to be working in our favor. Let's think this through carefully, but Jimmy is our priority. I've got some work to do. Let me hang on to this letter."

"Fine. Make me a copy, though. I want to show it to Hubert. Then I need to buy a red cap and make sure I have a clean blue shirt. Plus, I'll need to make sure my truck is ready by Thursday. I should drive up on Thursday if I'm going to be there for breakfast at six-thirty on Friday."

"You are way ahead of me on this, aren't you?" Jason said, as he turned to his copy machine and made a single copy of Ricky's surprising letter. He started to hand the copied letter to Adam but hesitated. "Are you sure you want to do this, Adam?"

"Let's not mess things up by breaking their rules. There's a ten-year-old boy out there who's a lot like me. We'd both love to see things get back to normal," Adam said, as he folded his copy of the letter and placed it in his shirt pocket. "I'm going to see if I can track down Hubert. Thanks, Jason."

7

Bluebird Diner

On Thursday, Operation Bluebird was set in motion. County Sheriff Bartlow was a practical, no-nonsense lawman. He agreed to let Adam be the Bluebird Diner point man. He saw it as a low-risk, tactical option and, if Adam was willing to do it, there was no reason to risk corrupting the plan with a substitute weed man. Adam was ready. His truck was ready.

Connie wasn't, though. If he hadn't had to drive north the night before, Friday could have passed as just another day at work, and she wouldn't have known the difference. All she knew was Adam was going back to Snyder. She knew nothing of what was at stake. He figured knowing wouldn't help her worry less. All he said was, "Connie, I'll be just fine. There is nothing to worry about. I've never tried to be a hero, and I'm not about to start now. I'm taking no chances. None."

As soon as he said it, he wished he hadn't. Denying he would take chances implied inherent risk. Rather than reinforce his denial and dig his unsettling hole deeper, he offered a loving and respectful ultimatum. He took her hand and said, "Connie, this is just one of those times you must trust me and smile, even if you don't feel like it."

He stayed at a neglected, five-cabin motel near the cafe that night, and he was the first customer through the door at the Bluebird Diner Friday morning. He sat in the windowed booth nearest the door and ordered scrambled eggs, bacon, wheat toast, and coffee. Ordering less didn't make sense, even though his nervous stomach suggested otherwise. Why wait for the cafe doors to open, only to order a donut and a cup of coffee? He wanted to look normal. His red hat remained on his head, even though that was not normal for Adam. Minutes after he sat down, a pickup stopped in front of the cafe and a young boy got out and retrieved a bundle from the truck's bed. Adam stopped buttering his toast and watched the entry as the boy approached. Adam resumed buttering. It was the paperboy. He placed a stack of newspapers on the counter and gave the waitress a quick wave. Adam walked to the counter, picked up a paper, and nodded to the waitress. Reading the news would settle his nerves and help him eat slowly as he waited.

The diner sat on a wide-open stretch of two-lane highway on the outskirts of town, and too much traffic on that lonely road would have been noticed. Most of the parking was directly in front of the restaurant. There was overflow parking to the west side of the building, but this wasn't an overflow time of day. Railroad tracks occupied the space beyond the highway, so there was no place to hide or park a car without raising suspicion other than in the spaces out front, which were mostly empty.

Adam thought he was on his own, but he wasn't. A plain-clothes deputy visited the cafe about ten minutes until seven. He parked a dented blue Chevy sedan near the front door, entered, and sat at the counter. He ordered coffee and a short stack and read a newspaper, which he brought with him. Adam thought he was just another early-morning customer.

Adam sat quietly, ate a little, sipped his coffee, glanced at his paper, and looked out the window occasionally. The sun had not risen, but clear early light was upon them. It allowed an extended look down Highway 48. He took a bite of crisp bacon, asked the waitress for a coffee warm-up, looked out the window, and caught his breath. A small boy rode a bike on the shoulder of the road. He came from the west on the wrong side of the road toward the diner. He peddled hard, skidding on the loose gravel as he turned into the blacktopped drive and headed for the front door of the cafe. He jumped off his bike, let it drop, and was almost in the door before the bike hit the pavement. Jimmy walked straight to Adam's booth and sat down facing his red-hatted rescuer.

Adam spoke through a gentle smile. "Hello, I'll bet you're Jimmy Tedrow, aren't you?"

"Yes, sir," Jimmy panted, still winded from his arduous bike ride.

"Jimmy, my name is Adam. I'm here to take you home. Are you ready?

Jimmy's eyes were huge and tearful. "Yes, sir," he said. "Yes, sir."

Adam reached across the table and placed his large palm across Jimmy's small left hand. "How about a donut?" he asked.

"No, thank you," Jimmy said, wiping his eyes with his right sleeve.

"Okay, then. Let's go home." Adam stood up, placed payment and tip on the table, and waited for Jimmy to scoot out of the booth. He put his arm around the boy's shoulder and walked him to the pickup. As he walked, Adam scanned the parking lot and the span of highway that led to the cafe. Except for a dented blue Chevy, there wasn't a car or person in sight. He buckled Jimmy in, tossed the bike in the pickup bed, and headed east on Highway 48 toward Jimmy's house.

The undercover deputy exited the cafe just behind Adam and Jimmy and walked casually to his car. Once Adam pulled onto the highway, he started his car and followed at a protective, inconspicuous distance and radioed the sheriff to tell him Jimmy was on his way home. The recovery phase was a success.

It was seven o'clock when they began the quick thirteen-mile trip to Jimmy's house. Adam avoided unwarranted conversation and let Jimmy take the lead.

"Are you a cop?" Jimmy asked.

"No, I'm just a friend, a friend who doesn't think much of the Hudson brothers. How far did you ride your bike this morning?"

"Ricky said it would be about a half mile."

"You are a brave young man, Jimmy. That's a long bike ride on a dark morning. Ricky dropped you off, did he?"

"Yes. He was the nice one. The other two are scary. Especially Rufus."

"They scared me too, Jimmy," he said. He took his eyes off the road and looked straight at Jimmy when he said it. "I'm sorry I ever met 'em. I'll bet you are too."

"They do that to your eye?" Jimmy asked.

Adam had forgotten how rough he looked with his black eye and bandage." As a matter of fact, they did," he answered. Adam was surprised at the question, but he wasn't going to lie to Jimmy, as he had to his grandchildren. Jimmy already knew how nasty people could be. "How'd you know?"

"I didn't know. I just guessed."

"You'd make a good detective, Jimmy. There's one thing that we don't have to guess about this morning though. You have two people waiting for you in Snyder who will be extremely glad to see you."

"I'll be glad to see them, too."

As they neared Snyder, he put Jimmy to work guiding him to the Tedrow home. Adam knew the way but wanted to keep Jimmy's mind in the moment if he could. It was a memorable reunion. Sheriff Bartlow, Deputy Hargrove, and Jason Salisbury waited with Jimmy's parents, Keith and Becky Tedrow, on the front porch of the small, well-kept bungalow. Adam parked his white pickup in front of the home with the passenger side of the pickup facing the house.

Jimmy popped his seat belt and was ready to bolt as soon as the pickup stopped. He unlatched the door and pushed it open wide with his feet and hit the ground running. He met his parents in the middle of the front yard and became the centerpiece of a three-person, swaying embrace. It caused the men to stand speechless and misty eyed in the face of undiluted joy. Later, Adam said everyone expected an emotional moment, but they had no idea how utterly powerful it would be. Keith Tedrow finally broke ranks with his family and headed straight for Adam. The indebted father grabbed Adam's hand and pulled him into a robust embrace of gratitude. No words were necessary.

Jimmy, his parents, and Salisbury went inside while Adam hoisted the bicycle from the pickup bed. As he did, the dented blue Chevy rolled to a stop behind Adam's pickup. The plainclothes deputy stepped from the car, smiled, and tipped his hat. "Hello, Adam. I'm Deputy McCallister," he said, offering his hand. "Thanks for letting me join you for breakfast. Nice job this morning."

Adam went from curious, to surprised, to grateful in the span of a handshake. "I'll be darned. You were at the Bluebird weren't you. I had no idea. Great to know you had my back. Thank you.?"

Sheriff Bartlow and Deputy Hargrove hastily crossed the yard toward Adam and Deputy McCallister. "Okay, it's time for phase two," Sheriff Bartlow said. "Adam, please join us inside. Hargrove, you take the squad. McCallister, drive your Chevy. You know what to do. And use your radios. Talk to each other but don't overdo it. Sam Bingham agreed to take up his crop duster for ariel surveillance. He'll be on your frequency. If he sees something, he'll tell ya." The two deputies were to scour the evenly sectioned countryside on the west side of Elwood in a five-square-mile swath. "They may be long gone. Or they could be holed up somewhere. We don't know. See anything fishy, call me. Radio's on my hip."

As the deputies drove away, Adam rolled Jimmy's bike across the yard, set the kickstand, placed the bike near the front steps, and followed the sheriff inside. The joy of Jimmy's return continued. And the questions lingered. Common sense made them wait to be answered. Jason Salisbury set the agenda.

"This is one happy ending that none of us will ever forget. Welcome home, Jimmy, welcome home. You have given us all a lesson in courage. And Mr. and Mrs. Tedrow, thank you for patience, and thank you for trusting us. You have been strong under incredibly tough circumstances. We're going to leave you alone for a while so you can catch your breath. But I'm sure you understand that we will need to talk with Jimmy later this morning." Jason checked his watch. "We'll go huddle up at the Snyder Cafe, and a couple of us will circle back here in about an hour. How's that sound?"

"That's fine." Keith Tedrow said. "You've got more work to do, don't you?"

"Yes, we do," answered Jason. "Is that okay with you, Jimmy?"

Jimmy let go of his mother's hand, walked over to Adam. "Are you coming back?"

Adam glanced at Jason, who gave him a quick, affirmative nod. Jason knew that if a quick friendship had developed between the boy and his rescuer, it could make the upcoming interview much easier.

"Yes, Jimmy. I'll be here. I wouldn't miss it. We've both met the Hudsons close up, haven't we?"

Jimmy nodded and returned to his mother's side.

8

The Cutting Board

THE CAFE MEETING IN downtown Snyder didn't go unnoticed by the locals. Three strangers, one a full-fledged sheriff, drinking coffee at the local diner was cause for whispered interest and speculation.

The three men sat in the booth farthest away from the counter and were mindful to talk softly. Their meeting was productive. Adam reported on his short ride with Jimmy. He thought it was vital that they know Jimmy referred to Ricky Hudson as "nice" and to his brothers as "scary." It was also important that they know that Ricky Hudson had been within a half mile of the Bluebird Diner less than two hours earlier.

Jason Salisbury explained his plan for the interview. "Please let me take the lead, gentlemen. You will have questions, but please limit them. Too many questions from too many people can confuse and sidetrack. If you have questions relevant to my direction, ask them. But, please, stay focused." He checked his watch and finished his coffee. "Time to go. I think we've given the Tedrows enough time to decompress."

The living room of the modest bungalow was quickly rearranged for the interview. A divan and chairs encircled the coffee table. Jimmy sat on the couch, next to his Mother. Adam sat nearest Jimmy's end of the divan in a side chair. Keith sat between Sheriff Bartlow and Jason on the opposite side of the coffee table, facing his son. Jason, with a fresh yellow legal pad on his lap and a pen in his hand, asked the first question.

"Jimmy, I hope you've had time to rest just a little," Jason said. This shouldn't take too long. We just need your input so we can have a better chance of catching these guys. Do you remember where you were when they took you?"

"Yes, sir. I rode my bike out by Heritage Park. There's a pond down there, and I was giggin' frogs. Just started when the one named Rufus grabbed me and threw me in that short back seat of his pickup. Ricky was in the back too. It was crowded."

"What time of day was that, Jimmy?" Jason asked.

"It was almost dark. That's the best time to gig frogs. You hear 'em croak. Then you shine a light on 'em and stick 'em."

"I guess that was last Wednesday?"

"Yes, sir."

"A gig is a little spear, right?"

"Yes, sir."

What happened to your gig when they grabbed you?"

"Don't know. I dropped it, I guess."

"Gigging sounds like fun. You good at it?"

"I'm okay."

"Why do you figure Rufus Hudson grabbed you? You have any idea?"

"Ricky told me it was because he thought I seen them stealing tires."

"Did you see them stealing tires?"

"Well, there's a couple of parking spaces down at that end of the pond. I seen their truck over there, and I seen them changing tires on a car parked beside them. It looked like Puke Williams's car, but I didn't think nothing of it. I was giggin' frogs."

Jason paused, then asked, "Who's Puke Williams?"

"His real name is Emil. He parks down there by himself sometimes. It's at the very end of an old gravel road that ain't used much. He drinks a lot, and sometimes he pukes out the window of his car and makes a mess all over the door. That's why we call him Puke."

Adam cast a glance at Jimmy's mom. She noticed and answered with a long, slow blink and an unbelieving headshake. He returned an understanding smile.

"Was Emil there that night?" Jason asked.

"I didn't see him, but I wasn't really lookin'."

"So, after they had you in the pickup, did they leave immediately, or did they return to finish their work on Emil's car?"

"No, we left right away. One of 'em threw my bike in the back of the pickup along with two tires, and we left. We drove straight to their farm. They argued the whole time about why Rufus took me and what they were gonna do with me. Rufus finally got really mad and told everyone to shut up and let him think. Ricky told me later that Rufus gets that way sometimes when he drinks too much."

"You think he was drinking that night?"

"I didn't see him drinkin', but there were empty beer cans on the floor of the truck, so figured he was."

"What happened next?"

"When we got to the farm, they was still arguing outside the car, but I couldn't understand exactly what they was sayin', but I figure they was tryin' to decide what to do with me. Then Harley and Ricky came and got me. They took me to the barn. They stuck me up in the hayloft and chained me to a pole that went all the way to the ceiling. I had that chain tight around my leg. I couldn't move around much. If I did, it hurt. The next day they took the chain off and kept me up there by taking down the hayloft ladder. Without the ladder, there was no way for me to get down. The hayloft was high, but I was glad to move around a little."

Adam interrupted. "Jimmy, would you mind if we looked at your leg?"

Jimmy pulled up his right pant leg and exposed the skin just above the ankle bone. It was slightly bruised but was not cut.

Jason paused a moment. Then he asked Becky Tedrow if he could trouble her for a glass of water. When she left, Jason asked Jimmy if they had hurt him in any other way. He wondered if they had hit him or slapped him or pinched him or done any other thing that caused him pain or concern.

"Nope. They just chained me up and left me to sleep in the hay. On the second day, Ricky brought me an air mattress, which was nice, but we left the next day. He was also the one who brought me food, and a couple times he stayed and talked with me for a while. He told me he was friends with you in high school, Dad. Did you know him?"

Becky returned with the water for Jason and asked if anyone else would like some. Everyone declined, and she took her place on the couch. Jimmy scooted close and stretched to whisper something in his Mother's ear.

"Sure," she said. "You go right ahead."

Jimmy jumped off the couch and headed for the bathroom.

Jason looked at Keith Tedrow and asked, "Did Jimmy explain all this to you earlier?

"Most of it. Nothing he told us this morning was much different, though he didn't mention Emil William's nickname, and he didn't tell us Ricky Hudson fed him and kept him company."

"Did it surprise you that he knew Emil Williams by name?"

"Everybody in town knows Emil Williams. Even the kids."

Keith teared up and took a deep breath. He hesitated, recovered his composure, and said, "Man, it is so easy to forget what it's like to be ten years old. They see so much, and we sit here totally oblivious. Gigged frogs and town drunks and crazed, lowlife Pikers and who knows what else. God forgive us."

Adam said, "Nobody blames you for this, Keith. Not us. Not Jimmy. Not anybody. You shouldn't either. I doubt that you had anything to do with what made the Hudson boys so vulgar and offensive, did you?"

"No, I can't say that I did," Keith said with a wistful smile.

Jimmy returned, hopped up on the couch. "Dad, did you know Ricky in high school?

"I knew him, but I didn't know him well. I remember having shop class with him."

"He said you was nice to him."

"I did him a favor once. Seems he never forgot. He didn't have many friends because he wasn't around very much."

"What sort of a favor?" Jimmy asked. He sat toward the front edge of the couch.

"Ricky and I shared the same table with four other guys. We all made laminated cutting boards. So, there we sat, three to a side, at that long worktable. We had our freshly finished cutting boards in front of us. Except for Ricky. His cutting board was missing, which surprised me because he worked hard to perfect it. The teacher would inspect each of them, one at a time, and give us our grade on the spot.

"Before he came to our table, I asked Ricky where his board was, and he said his big brother had smashed it with a hammer. I asked him why and he just shrugged. He said, 'Sometimes he can be pretty mean.'

"We sat facing each other on opposite sides of the table. Mr. Cox checked my side first and then stepped away. I pushed my cutting board across the table so it sat directly in front of Ricky." Keith slowly pushed an imaginary cutting board across the coffee table toward Jimmy.

"Mr. Cox came back and inspected Ricky's side of the table and didn't know the difference. I remember it well because I got a B and he got an A on the same darned cutting board. We laughed about it a lot after that. He wasn't what I'd call a high school buddy, but I got along with him. Like I said, he was never around much."

"If he's the one who freed Jimmy, I'd say he's returned the favor and then some," Sheriff Bartlow said.

"How about that, Jimmy?" Jason asked. "For whatever reason, Ricky seemed to want to send you home. Did he and his brothers argue about that?"

"I don't know. I wasn't around them when they were together, except on the first day when they put me in the pickup and then when we left their farm. And that ride was real quiet, and they made me lay on the floor."

"Where did they take you when you left their place?" Jason asked.

"I don't know. They blindfolded me, threw my bike in the back, and drove for a long time, maybe more than an hour. Then they stopped at a place that seemed like another farm. They took me inside and shut me in an empty bedroom. They threw in a blanket. That's all. I missed the air mattress."

"Did they remove your blindfold?" Jason asked.

"I did that." Jimmy said through a partially arrested yawn. He scooted toward the back of the couch cushion and closer to his mother. She put her arm around him and stared patiently at Jason.

Jason understood. "Jimmy, we're almost done. Just the same, it may be a good time to take a little break." Jason, stood, stretched, finished his glass of water, and asked if anyone needed to stretch their legs. Nobody did. Then he asked, "Jimmy, suppose you could teach me to gig frogs?"

"You seem plenty smart enough to learn," Jimmy said.

The room was silent for a moment while the humor in Jimmy's innocent remark landed. Jason Salisbury broke into laughter followed by the rest of the room. Everybody laughed, including Jimmy, once he realized he'd said something funny. He wasn't sure why it was funny, but he laughed. It felt good to laugh.

"Jimmy, I may just take you up on that." The short break and the shared laughter seemed to refresh everyone. "But, for now, I'd better stick to business. No kidding, Jimmy. We are about done. Just a few more questions. Are you okay with that?" Jason asked as he returned to his chair.

"Okay," Jimmy said.

"Let's go back to that place where they took you. They stuck you in a bedroom. How'd you know it was a bedroom?"

"Just seemed like it. There were light places on the walls where pictures had been, and an empty closet off to the side. There was a window, but I couldn't get it open."

"Great that you tried, Jimmy. Just great." Jason said. "When you were in there, could you hear them talking?"

"I heard voices, but I couldn't understand what they was sayin'. They weren't in the very next room."

"Was there anyone else there? I mean, did you hear a voice that sounded new or different?"

"No."

Jason flipped the page on his legal pad and eased his intensity. "What'd they give you to eat? Anything good?"

"When I was in the barn, they brought me scrambled eggs and stuff. But at the new place, it was mostly snacks: beef jerky, them chewy nut-bars, apples, and pop mostly. Ricky did give me a cold hotdog and chocolate milk on the day we got to the new place. But it was mostly snack stuff."

"When you had the hotdog, did you notice where it came from. I mean, was there a label on the sack?"

"I don't think so. At least, I don't remember none."

"You say it seemed like another farm. What makes you say that?"

"It smelled like a farm. And it was real quiet, except for the crickets. I could hear 'em chirpin' as soon as they turned off the truck."

"What does a farm smell like, Jimmy."

"Cow manure. This one did, anyway."

"This morning, when they brought you to the Bluebird Diner, how long a drive was it? Do you remember how long it took to get from that farm to the place they released you?"

Jimmy shrugged. "I guess it was a half hour or so. Seemed long, probably 'cause I was blindfolded again."

"They talk at all during that ride?"

"Not much. Only in the beginning. When we left, Ricky asked Rufus how far we had to go. Rufus called him a bad name and told him we'd get there when we got there."

Jason flipped the scribbled pages of his legal pad back to their original position, clicked his ballpoint twice, and said, "Jimmy, you are a brave young man. It is nice to have you home. I don't think any of us could have been held captive by three strange men for over a week and come home as calm and collected as you are. What's your secret?" asked Jason.

"No secret. But it helped to stay mad. Seemed like bein' mad helped me not cry. I cried the first night because I was lonely and scared in that barn all by myself. But I just got mad and stopped. I didn't cry again till I saw Mr. Thompson sittin' in that booth in his red ball cap. I don't know why I cried then. I just did."

There was an abrupt knock at the door, and Deputy Hargrove opened the door and took one step inside the small foyer.

"Excuse me, everybody, but I found something on the road just past Elwood that you will want to see," the deputy said.

"What did you find?" asked Sheriff Bartlow, slightly miffed because of the interruption.

"Ricky Hudson. He's in the car."

"What? Where in the hell did you find him?"

"We finished our country-road search. Found nothing. Sam saw some dusty-road traffic from his plane. Two hay trucks and a Jeep, but no red pickup. So, we turned around and drove back real slow on the highway. I led in the squad. We stayed about a quarter mile apart so if one of 'em jumped from the ditch behind me, McCallister'd see 'em. About two miles this side of Elwood, there he was. Just walking along the road. Not hidin' at all. He offered no resistance. It was almost like he was glad to see me."

"I need to talk to him," Sheriff Bartlow said.

9

The Red Cap

SHERIFF BARTLOW WAS OUT the door before his deputy could turn around. He ran to the squad car. Deputy McCallister had parked his blue Chevy close behind the squad. Deputy Hargrove followed at an unhurried pace. He knew Ricky Hudson was cuffed and securely locked inside the squad car, and he knew his casual saunter would allow him to extend his moment in the sun.

The others also hurried to the porch to see Hargrove's trophy. Ricky sat locked in the squad car, peering through the back seat window nearest the house. He saw Jimmy and offered a hesitant, handcuffed wave. Jimmy tried to return the gesture, but his mother grabbed his hand and brought it to his side quickly. He gave Ricky a quick smile and held onto his mother's hand.

Sheriff Bartlow circled the car, checking the locks and climbed in the front seat on the passenger's side. He threw his left arm atop the bench seat and spoke with his prisoner for about five minutes before he returned to the house. Hargrove stayed by the car during the interview, leaning against the back fender closest to Ricky's window. Adam thought it looked like he was posing for a picture.

"It's him, alright. He said his brothers ditched him," the sheriff said as he approached the porch steps. "They parked about a mile away from the restaurant. Ricky walked Jimmy and his bike about halfway there and let him go the rest of the way on his own. When Ricky went back, they were gone. He didn't know where they might have gone, but I think if we lean on him a little, he might remember something. But, for now, we must get him into a cell. We've got a small holding cell tucked in behind the Shell station in Snyder, but I think we had better take him to Spring Valley and book him properly."

"Glad I'm riding with you," Jason said. "It'll give me a chance to talk to him. Did you read him his rights?"

"First thing I did."

"Should be an interesting ride home. But I need to wrap things up here first. Can you give me five minutes?"

"Sure," Sheriff Bartlow said. "Do what you need to do. Hargrove, keep an eye on Ricky, will you? And tell McCallister to head back to Spring Valley. Have him tell the boys at the jail to make room for Ricky, but to talk to absolutely no one else about this until we get back."

Adam, Jason, the sheriff, and the Tedrows went back inside and took their places in the circle of chairs surrounding the coffee table. Jason spoke first.

"Well, things happen kinda fast sometimes, don't they? As you said, Keith, we still have some work to do, but it appears that it just became a little easier. We still have some questions, but I'll bet Ricky's going to answer most of them. We may need to talk with you again, Jimmy. We will, of course, keep in touch either way.

"There is something else. The world deserves to know that Jimmy's home. We'll release that information later today. Unfortunately, that means you will probably have some media folks contacting you. First, please know you don't have to talk to any of them. Simply ask them to respect your privacy and refer them to me. Here's a half dozen of my cards. If you choose to talk to them, the two of you do the talking. Don't let Jimmy talk to the press because he's a witness. And give them no details. Jimmy is home. That's the story. Why he was kidnapped and why he was released are uncertain.

"We don't mean to tie your hands, but too much available information could slow our search. The less they know about what we know, the better. This is a lot to digest, I know. Just know that we are still with you on this. If you have any questions or concerns, call me, please. How about questions right now? Do you have any?"

"Not now," Keith said. "I'm sure I'll think of something the minute you leave."

"Please. Call me if you do. One more thing. Do you have a doctor?"

"Yes, Doc Olsen over in Elwood." Keith said.

"Take Jimmy to see him today. We want to make sure he's as healthy as he appears to be. Give the doctor my card and have him send me the bill. You say his name is Olsen?"

"Yes."

"I'll have someone call him today to confirm. But get him to a doctor as soon as you can. Okay? We've still got some work to do, but what's important is Jimmy's home where he belongs.

Everyone but Jimmy stood and traded handshakes. Jason stopped in front of Jimmy. "Jimmy, you are one tough cookie. We are proud of you. Welcome home! He extended his hand. Jimmy shook it and smiled. He was happy Jason was leaving.

"Adam, I'll see you tomorrow. And thanks for a fantastic job today."

"It's a morning we won't forget. Right, Jimmy?" Adam smiled at Jimmy as he spoke. He started to follow Jason and Sheriff Bartlow out the door. Then he stopped, turned around, walked back to Jimmy, and placed his red ball cap on Jimmy's head. "Hang onto that for me, will you? It'll give me a reason to come back and see you. I'll take you out for a real breakfast." He placed a business card on the coffee table, smiled at Jimmy's parents, and walked out the door to his white, government-issued pickup.

10

Kathy

NINE DAYS HAD PASSED since Adam first set foot in Snyder. In that short period, he had met the Hudson brothers, driven into a Piker's trap, gotten four stitches in his forehead, and helped rescue a kidnapped child. His formula for happiness was simple. If he had things seventy-five percent familiar and twenty-five percent strange, he'd be content. In recent days, that ratio was reversed. He wanted to decompress. He'd start with a visit with the Snyder grocer.

Kathy Burns was restocking the bread rack when she heard him enter the store. She recognized Adam and his healing black eye immediately.

"Well, look who's here. How's your noggin?" she asked.

"It's healing. I'm fine. I just wanted to say thanks before I head back home," he said. "I honestly don't know what I would have done if you hadn't patched me up and then hurried me over to Doc Olsen's. So, thank you."

"Well, you was bleedin' all over my front counter, you know," she said, deflecting his compliment. "But what are you doing here? Was you with that bunch that was over at the cafe this mornin'? Did you help rescue Jimmy Tedrow?" Kathy asked.

"Yeah, I was a small part of it. How'd you find out about it so fast?"

"Oh, Deputy Hargrove was over there braggin' about it a while ago. Was it really the Hudson brothers who had him?"

"I'm afraid it was. I think it's safe to say that you won't have to worry about them stealing chewing gum for a while anyway."

"How'd you get involved. I thought you said you wasn't a cop."

"Wrong place at the right time, I guess. You know, if I had taken your advice and steered clear of the Hudsons, I could have avoided a bunch of trouble. You are a smart lady. Of course, if I'd done that, Jimmy Tedrow might still be missing. Sometimes I think the good Lord lets us make dumb decisions for a reason. You ever get down to Spring Valley?"

"Sometimes."

"Give me a call if you feel like it. My wife and I would love to take you to the best fried chicken restaurant in the county," Adam said. He placed his business card on the counter, rapped his knuckles twice, and said, "Thanks again. Thank Bradly for me, too." He left the store. He had one more stop to make.

He drove north to the Hudson place. He wanted to take a final look at the cattle guard. He stopped his pickup in front of the reassembled gate. The pipe grid covered the ditch, and the skid rail was empty. He stepped out of the pickup, took a picture and was on his way home, eager to share the second chapter of his unusual story with his family.

Deep Thinker

IT WAS DUSK. RUFUS and Harley rested on the living room floor of the vacant farmhouse where they had holed up for most of the last four days. They sat side by side, leaning against the wall with their legs stretched before them on the dusty floor, which was cluttered with snack-food wrappers and empty beer and pop cans.

"Rufus, I miss Ricky. He musta been heart broke when we left him behind," Harley said.

"Harley, I miss him too, but it's best for him, and its best for us," Rufus answered.

"Why is it best for him and best for us?"

"Cause Ricky's soft and he ain't dependable. Sometimes he's with us. Sometimes he ain't. He laughed harder than both of us when we put that weed man in the ditch." Rufus wadded an empty jerky package, tossed it in the air, and batted it across the room.

"But you know how he gets around strangers. Has to cozy up to people all the time. Wants to make friends and talk. Always reminds me of that old Lab dog we used to have. Spike. Remember him? Couldn't have a visitor without the damned dog jammin' his nose in their crotch till they scratched his ear. Ricky's the same goddammed way."

Rufus turned and looked straight at Harley and kept talking. "Look how fast he made friends with that boy. Claimed he knew his dad in high school and felt bad about takin' the kid. That's his problem. He's always lookin' for friends and for something better 'cause Dad let him go to school. He ain't never been satisfied with his life with us. Never gonna be. Besides, he had it easy. You and me, we was workin' when we was twelve. Truth is, our pansy-assed, little brother would just slow us down, and he'd totally hate bein' on the run. Do you understand?"

"I guess."

"Well, good. Now, quit your goddamned harpin' about it."

"Suppose he's in jail or still hidin' somewhere?"

"I suppose they got him by now, which is why we're getting' out of here. About now he's givin' them a good idea where we are. I don't think he knew for sure. I drove around a while just to mix up the kid. Probably mixed Ricky up some too."

Rufus was the only one who knew exactly where they hid out. He knew because he made it his business to know about things like the location of vacant houses and distressed property. He bought and sold many of them. Other times he was a "finder," bringing buyers and sellers together for much less than a licensed real estate agent could. He was an opportunistic bottom-feeder who knew who was selling out or moving out or just having a hard time making ends meet. That's how he knew that Fred Shultz and his family had sold the farm and quietly moved to California. That's how he knew that Lloyd Freeze had bought the place but didn't live there and hadn't begun to work it yet. And that's how Rufus saved nearly fifty thousand dollars, five thousand of which was tucked in a bulging money bag sewn inside the bib on his overalls. The rest remained hidden in the kitchen of the Hudson farmhouse.

"We'll leave after dark. They know what we're drivin' so we can't travel during the day."

"Where we goin', Rufus?"

"Where do you want to go?"

"I don't know," Harley said. "Where can we go?"

"Just about anywhere, except home."

After a thoughtful, downcast moment, Harley's mood brightened. "I always wanted to see that place they got them presidents faces carved in that mountain."

"You mean Mount Rushmore?"

"That's it."

"Well then, that's where we'll go."

"Rufus, can I ask you something without you gettin' mad?"

"I guess."

"Do you ever wish you hadn't took that boy?"

Rufus hesitated. He drummed the fingers of his right hand on the dusty floor several times and stared across the room at the faded wallpaper. "Well, it seemed like the right thing to do at the time, and I know things would be a lot simpler now if I hadn't took him. But, damn it, we been helpin' ourselves to stuff from people's cars, houses, and barns pretty regular lately. Don't want that all to come back and bite us. The stupid little shitass kid shouldn't have been there watchin' us.

"Couldn't keep him though. Keepin him would've been trouble and plenty of it. That's why I agreed to Ricky's plan to turn him loose. And, if we'd kept him, we woulda had to keep Ricky. We can move a lot better without the both of them. Just think, tomorrow or the next day we'll get to see Mount Rushmore. Isn't that something?"

"Yeah. Be nice if Ricky could see it too."

Rufus took a slow, exasperated breath and released it with a disgusted sigh. "Shut up about Ricky. I ain't goin' to tell you again!"

"I got one more question."

"One more, Harley, and that's all. You're gettin' on my nerves."

"Why didn't Dad let us go to school like Ricky?"

"I don't know for sure. Coulda been the times. Remember, he's ten years younger than you and twelve years younger than me. Always figured times was tougher when we was kids, and Dad needed us to work. Then I asked him one time why Ricky didn't have to work like we did. He said that he just saw something in Ricky that needed educatin', so he let him go to school. Then, like a goddamned idiot, I asked him what he saw in me. He just laughed real loud with his mouth wide open, like he done sometimes. You know how he did. He'd let ya see the tobacco slobber hanging from his teeth. Well, he told me I was just like him. He said I was mean as hell, and that bein' mean would get me by better than some damned education."

"Remember what he said about me?" Harley asked. Then he answered his own question. "He said no one should call me an idiot. He said I was a deep thinker, and deep thinkers just think a little slower than other folks."

"I remember, Harley. You are a deep thinker." Rufus said. He got up from the dusty floor, kicked an empty Coke can across the room, and walked to the unadorned window. He gazed into the dark evening. His rare moment of reflection was over.

"Hey, Harley, what are the names of the six presidents on Mount Rushmore?

"I don't know."

"Well, let's go find out."

1 2

Peeking at Evil

ADAM USED THE SHELL station payphone to call Connie. He told her he would be home in an hour or so. He chose not to give her the whole story. All he said was, "Mom, you've heard about the Tedrow boy kidnapping, right?" She said, of course, she had. "Well, I can't give you all the details right now, but I helped rescue him. That's where I've been. The Hudson brothers had him, and we got him back. I'll tell you all about it when I get home."

"The Hudson brothers? You mean the same guys that cut your head?"

"The same," he said. "Give Mike a call and asked him to come over so I can tell you all about it. I should be home by five-thirty for sure. Connie, just one more thing."

"What's that?" she asked.

"I love you," he said. "I'll see you in a bit.

Mike and Molly were both there when Adam got home. They left the kids with a neighbor because they wanted an uninterrupted opportunity to hear his story.

Three smiling faces greeted him as he walked in the back door. Connie, Mike, and Molly sat at the kitchen table and broke into a steady round of applause as he entered the room. Connie stopped clapping first, got up, and wrapped her husband in a wholehearted embrace.

Mike spoke first. "You predicted an exciting second chapter. Sounds like you've kept your promise. Use the bathroom if you need to, put on your slippers if you want to, grab a beer if you want to, but sit down and tell us all about it. You are a legend in your own time."

"Oh, I'm sorry, but you'll have to wait. I'm expecting a call from Dan Rather and CBS News. I'm sure you understand," he teased before he opened a beer and joined them at the table. He leaned over and kissed Molly on the cheek and then began talking. He gave them almost every detail, from Ricky's letter to the red-capped meet-up with Jimmy Tedrow at the Bluebird Diner. He covered the thrill of the Tedrow reunion, Puke Williams's tires, and the casual capture of Ricky Hudson. "It was a day I'll never forget."

"That is an incredible story. Why do you think Ricky Hudson invited you to be the man to meet Jimmy?" Mike asked.

"I think it was more coincidental than anything. I left them two business cards when I visited their farm, so my number was handy. Also, they knew I was a government guy, but I wasn't a cop. I think that made a difference. We may learn more from Ricky as we talk with him."

"As 'we' talk to him? What do you mean by 'we'? You are not still involved in the hunt for the other brothers, are you?" Mike asked.

"Oh, no, but they'll keep me posted, I'm sure. I'll be back to work soon enough. I was there by accident, of course, but sometimes you live through events that sort of bind you to people, ya know. I'll bet this was just as big a deal for Jason Salisbury and Hubert St. John as it was for me."

"I'm sure you're right. And what you did took courage. It's just that I'm not used to you working a dangerous job. That's something we'll have to get used to," Mike said.

"Oh, no, we won't," Connie said. "He's out of the crime-solving business, plain and simple. I am proud of you, Adam, but chasing bad weeds is different than chasing bad men. The past few days are days that I don't want to live through again."

"I doubt that you'll have to, Mom," Adam said.

Molly got up, circled the table, and hugged her father-in-law. Her head nestled close to his ear, and she whispered, "Nice job, Dad. And, you know what? I am not surprised."

Mike called Scott later that night and reported what happened. They talked for almost an hour. By the time they hung up, Mike had repeated the story in shuffled increments at least three times. The kidnapping story broke in the Omaha World-Herald and the Spring Valley Sentinel the next day. Adam was identified only as an affiliated government employee. Family members all bragged about Adam's participation, even Connie. "Hey," she said to Ralph, the butcher at the Sixth Street Market. "Did you see the story about the Tedrow kidnapping?"

"Sure did," Ralph answered.

"Do you know who the affiliated government employee was who help with the rescue?"

"No."

"It was Adam."

"Your Adam?"

"My Adam. Quite a story behind it. I'll tell you about it when you're not working."

There came a time when they stopped bragging. The news traveled too fast. Pastor Gerber called to confirm the story and to see if things were alright. The mailman mentioned it. People they didn't even know wanted to talk to them about "Adam's heroism."

"First of all, there was no heroism about it. It was an adventure. That's for sure, but I just did what seemed to be the right thing," Adam insisted. "I think people are just curious about the dark side, and, when they know someone who has flirted with it, they want to get close. It's a safe way to peek at evil. At least, that's how it seems to me."

Because of his job, Jason Salisbury knew more about the dark side than Adam. After his ride back to Spring Valley with Ricky Hudson, he said he was reminded there are different degrees of darkness. He said that Ricky was dead-to-rights guilty in the eyes of the law, but a reasonable measure of common sense might modify the depth of his guilt in the eyes of many. The evil seemed to reside in Rufus, not Ricky. Harley remained an enigma.

~~~~~~

Rufus and Harley pulled into a twenty-four-hour Waffle House in Rapid City about 4:30 a.m. An ancient waitress, wrapped in a checkered Waffle House apron, took their order. Rufus ordered a waffle, bacon, and coffee. After a little coaxing from Rufus, Harley ordered the Waffle Supreme, which came bedecked with strawberries and whipped cream. Their waitress noticed Harley's eyes light up when she placed the plate before him and asked. "How about a little more whipped cream? I think they shorted you a little." She left before he could answer and returned with an uncapped can of Reddi Whip. She smiled and added a small mountain of white fluff to his already well-trimmed waffle.

"Damn, Harley," said Rufus, "Sure you can eat all that?"

"I'm sure. This is good," Harley answered, as he spread the whipped cream across the square hollows in his waffle and licked his fork. "This is real good."

"Been a while since we ate out, ain't it?" Rufus said.

"Yeah. This is good. Real good."

"Well, eat up. We gotta find a place to sleep for a while before we see the presidents."

"Wonder if Ricky ever had a waffle like this?" Harley asked.

Rufus exploded. He slammed both fists on the tabletop. Coffee splashed from the full cups. The little metal syrup pitcher bounced and fell on its side. Salt and pepper shakers rattled but stayed upright. Harley stopped chewing and stared at Rufus, whose fists rested before him on the messed table.

"Goddamned idiot! Will you shut up about Ricky?" Rufus said, in an unrestrained whisper. "No more. One more mention of Ricky and I'll put so much whipped cream up your ass you'll shit chocolate marshmallows!"

"I forgot," Harley said. His eyes teared up, and he said, "But you called me an idiot. Daddy said that ain't right. He said I was a deep thinker and . . ."

"Deep thinkers just think a little slower than most," Rufus finished Harley's sentence, as he calmed a little. "I know, I know, but ya gotta help me think about what we're goin' to do next instead of daydreamin' about Ricky all the time."

"I thought we was goin' to see the presidents next," Harley said.

"Yeah, that's what we're doin' next, Harley. We're goin' to get some sleep and go see the presidents." Rufus motioned for the check and accepted the dreaded truth that was before him. His deep-thinking, younger brother would be a burden during a flight from the law.

The ancient waitress brought the check. "You boys alright?" she asked, as she stood ready to clean the table.

"We're fine," Rufus said. "Sorry about the mess." He dug two quarters out of his pocket for a tip, then paid the check.

The tired brothers checked into the Motel 6 just off Interstate 90 about six a.m. Rufus knew he was taking a chance by staying at a cut-rate motel because it was probably where his pursuers would expect him to stay. He checked in anyway. He was too tired to consider other options. He paid cash for two nights just in case he needed them. The unshaven fugitives parked their pickup behind the building and found their room on the second floor. Room 222 was just one door away from the ice machine. Both men took off their boots, sprawled on the beds, and slept soundly until about 11 a.m., when they were awakened by the annoying clatter of ice being scooped into a cooler.

"Harley, you awake?" Rufus asked.

"Yeah."

"Feeling okay?"

"Yeah. Been nice to sleep a little more."

"You go ahead and do that or watch TV if you want to. Bet there's somethin' good on. Cartoons or somethin'. I gotta go shoppin'. Seen a Walmart not far from here. I'll go get us new shirts and some other stuff," Rufus explained.

"Can I go with you?" asked Harley.

"No, not this time. The cops are lookin' for two guys in a red Toyota pickup. Better if you stay here. Then there'll be just one guy in the red Toyota pickup. Pretty tricky, huh?

"Yeah, pretty tricky. Pretty tricky."

"I'll be back before you know it. Promise me now. You will not leave this room. Okay? Not for any reason.

"I'll stay right here, Rufus. I promise."

Rufus didn't doubt that Harley would stay put, and Walmart had everything he needed to create a necessary Hudson brother transformation. Around their hometown, remaining scruffy offered an intimidating advantage. The advantage was now a liability. They needed to blend in rather than frighten. A shower, a shave, new plaid shirts, crisp jeans and overalls, and new shoes significantly changed their first-impression appearance. Harley got the jeans and white tennis shoes. Rufus got the overalls and new boots. He also bought a sewing kit so that he could affix the money bag inside the bib of his new overalls. They became ordinary, blue-collar men on vacation rather than disheveled men on the run.

Harley was pleased. Rufus was too, but for a different reason. When he attached the money bag to his new overalls and emptied the bib pocket of his old ones, he found something that completed his plan for Harley—a business card for the noxious weed supervisor of Frederick County. His plan would wait. Today, they would visit the presidents.

Two men in a red pickup drove into the Black Hills and on to Mount Rushmore. In addition to new clothing, their red truck had new South Dakota license plates, stolen from a car in the Walmart parking lot. The Nebraska plates rested beneath the front seat. The scenery was spectacular.

1 3

Along for the Ride

"Ricky, we've found the farmhouse where you and your brothers hid out. But that doesn't help us much, does it?" Jason Salisbury asked. "Do you have any idea where they may have gone?"

"No, sir. I don't. I didn't even know where the farmhouse was," Ricky Hudson answered. He sat, unshackled, clad in orange jailhouse pajamas. A guard stood just inside the interrogation room door.

Jason shifted in his seat and stared across the table at Ricky. They had spent nearly half an hour in the unadorned room with a two-way window. "Use your imagination now. Come on, you know your brothers better than anybody. Where would they go if they wanted to hide? Do you have friends or relatives somewhere they might turn to for help?"

"No friends or relatives. It's just us. Another vacant farmhouse, maybe. I don't know. Rufus knows a lot about that kind of stuff."

"Yes, we've learned that he bought and sold distressed homes in his spare time. Farming and real estate seem an odd combination. He make a lot of money doin' that?"

"Don't know. He always had some money, but I don't know where he got it. He held on to it unless there was somethin' he wanted really bad. Like a tractor. We came down here to Spring Valley once and bought a tractor. Don't think I ever seen him so happy. It was fun."

"Was he the only one who had money. How about Harley? Did he work anywhere off the farm? Did you?" Jason said.

"No. Would've been hard for Harley. He's sorta slow. Dad said he was a deep thinker, and deep thinkers think slower than other folks. Me? Rufus wouldn't let me go anywhere. He was afraid I'd make friends, I think. He wanted us to keep to ourselves."

"How about your Dad?" Jason asked. "He still living?"

"No. He died when I was fifteen. Climbed up a windmill somewhere up in Pike County. Fell off. Kid had a kite stuck in its blades. Dad climbed up to pry it loose, lost his footing, and fell. He died two days later. Did me a big favor before he died, though. He made Rufus promise to let me finish school. He was like Rufus, you know. Kind sometimes, mad sometimes. Mostly mad, though. Guess that's what makes the kind times stand out."

"How about your Mom?"

"Died when I was born."

"I'm sorry," Jason said, then paused a moment and continued. "As I told you, your story about the kidnapping pretty much matches what Jimmy Tedrow told us. You were just along for the ride. You didn't take Jimmy. Rufus did. And the things you did along the way, helped us find Jimmy. That is all good. So, if you continue to cooperate with us, things could be even better. So, think. Think hard about your brothers. Anything you can tell us that will help us find them will help you. It'll help them too. The sooner we find them, the safer they'll be. Think hard, Ricky. Think hard." Jason motioned for the guard to unlock the door, and he left the room.

Jason immediately met with Sheriff Bartlow, who had witnessed his conversation with Ricky from behind the two-way glass. "Well, we learned a little more about the Hudsons but nothing about where they might be. Harley seems like sort of an innocent bystander too."

"Being retarded don't get him off the hook," Sheriff Bartlow said.

"You mean mentally challenged, don't you?" Jason asked.

"Yeah, that too."

"Listen. Rufus bought and sold property. He had to deal with other people to do that. Find anybody you can who might have dealt with him. Title companies, banks, insurance companies, real estate guys, tax guys. Anybody who might have done business with him. We just need to know more about this guy. Also, check with the Frederick County appraiser. See if they can identify other vacant farmhouses in the county. Check up in Pike County too."

"We're on it, Jason."

Jason returned to his office and called Hubert St. John. "Hey, Hubert. I'm checking in. We just interrogated Ricky Hudson again. Didn't learn much about where they might be, but we did learn a little more about brother Harley. He's mentally challenged. My guess is he'll do just about anything big brother Rufus tells him to do."

"Rufus had his own little family fiefdom, didn't he? That's over now. Maybe that'll work to our advantage," Hubert answered.

"Say, how's Thompson doing?"

"He's back to work. His head is almost healed. His pickup is as good as new, but his moment in the sun is bugging the hell out of him. He likes normal, and having people quiz him about rescuing Jimmy isn't normal. It'll pass."

Normal would remain elusive for Adam Thompson. A day later, Adam received a surprising phone call from Rufus Hudson.

14

The Presidents

HARLEY LOVED MOUNT RUSHMORE. He spent three dollars' worth of quarters peering at the presidents through the coin-operated scenic viewer. Despite what he was about to do, Rufus enjoyed the afternoon too. They watched a twenty-minute video about how Gutzon Borglum and his son, Lincoln, carved the sixty-foot heads of Washington, Jefferson, Lincoln, and Roosevelt. They visited the gift shop, bought two Mount Rushmore T-shirts and some polished Black Hills rocks. They strolled around the grounds, enjoying the ever-present smell of ponderosa pine and the Black Hills spruce. At about six o'clock they began the thirty-minute ride back to Rapid City.

"Well, what did you think?" Rufus asked. "Was it what you expected?"

"It was big, wasn't it? Real big. Bigger than I thought. And how them guys made them faces is something. I ain't never seen something like that."

"Yeah, it is somethin'. I'm glad you liked it."

"Thanks for taking me, Rufus. I liked it a lot."

"Next time you see Ricky, you'll have to tell him all about it," Rufus said.

"I sure will. I sure will," Harley answered, then hesitated. "When we going to see Ricky?"

"I ain't sure. But we will."

They parked behind the motel and went to their room. "We're paid up for tonight," Rufus said. "Then we can head out tomorrow. I need to do a little runnin' around in the morning before we go. I want to see if I can get us another car."

"Okay," Harley said as he rolled the polished rocks around in his right hand. "These rocks is sure pretty."

They watched TV for a while, turned it off, and fell asleep. The ice machine was mercifully quiet. Rufus awoke at five-thirty a.m. He tried not to awaken Harley, but he was not successful. "Hey, Harley. Did you dream about them presidents?"

"I slept good, but I didn't dream about the presidents. I dreamed about Ricky."

"Can't much help what ya dream about, can ya?" Rufus asked. "Hey, how'd you like another whipped-cream waffle this morning?"

"That sounds good."

They sat in the same booth as their first visit. The waitress was different. She was younger. The checkered apron was the same, but it fit differently. Rufus ordered scrambled eggs. Harley ordered another Waffle Supreme, and Rufus asked for extra whipped cream for his brother.

"Harley, I want you to listen close. I got to find us a new car. We are pushing our luck driving that red pickup around. That means I will be gone most of the day. I want you to stay in the room at the motel until I get back. Can you do that?"

"Sure," Harley answered.

"We'll get some snacks and pop for you. Go down to get some ice if you want to. But don't go no further than that. You must stay in the room. Okay?"

"Sure. What kind of car you gettin'?"

"Not sure," said Rufus. "One more thing. When I get back, I'll knock on the door two times. Just two times. You'll say, 'Who's there?' Then I'll say Abraham Lincoln. That way, you'll know it's okay to open the door. Okay? Got that?"

"Yes, I got it. You knock two times. I say 'Who's there?' You say Abraham Lincoln and I open the door."

"That's right. You don't leave the room, except to get ice. Right? Now, repeat it all to me."

Harley repeated his instructions correctly with a slight smile at the mention of Abraham Lincoln and the thought of Mount Rushmore. Breakfast came. The young waitress didn't skimp on the whipped cream. She smiled as she placed his smothered waffle before him. Rufus allowed time for a leisurely breakfast, asking Harley to repeat his door-opening instructions several times as they finished eating and enjoyed their second cup of coffee.

Room 222 at Motel 6 on Interstate 90 in Rapid City, South Dakota, was well stocked with chips, granola bars, fruit, and Harley's favorite pop, Coke and A&W Root Beer. Harley relaxed on the bed watching television. Rufus paid for another day at the motel, drove the red pickup with stolen South Dakota plates straight to the bus depot, and bought a ticket to Denver. Then he got a pocket full of change and made a long-distance phone call to the noxious weed supervisor of Frederick County.

Adam was in his basement office planning his day. The phone rang at about 8:30 a.m., and he answered with only his name. "Thompson."

"You Adam Thompson, the Fredrick County weed man?" Rufus asked.

Adam recognized his voice immediately and tried not to stumble over his shock. "That's me. How can I help you?"

"This here's Rufus Hudson. You remember me?"

"Of course, Rufus. I remember you," Adam said. His voice did not reveal his surprise.

It's Harley I'm calling about. I want to send him home 'cause he ain't guilty, and he ain't cut out for bein' on the run. I need your help with that."

"My help? Doubt that I can help much. You should be talking to the sheriff."

"Maybe, but I ain't. I'm talking to you. Just listen a minute. You'll see it's real damned simple. You might want to write this down. You got a pen?"

Being alone with Rufus, even on the phone, was unsettling. He fumbled for a pen and notepad and took a deep breath to still his nervousness. "Okay, Rufus. I am ready," Adam said.

"Okay. Harley is in Rapid City, South Dakota. He's stayin' in the Motel 6 that's right off I-90. He's in room 222, and he's goin' to be there all day and tonight. You need to send somebody to get him. Now, he thinks I'm comin' back, and he ain't goin' to open the door to just anybody. So, whoever goes should knock on the door twice. No more. Just twice. Then he'll ask 'Who's there?' They should answer, 'Abraham Lincoln.' He'll open the door. That way, there'll be no fuss. Everyone can keep their guns in their holsters. No need to break the door down. It'll be smooth and easy. You got all that? Repeat it to me."

Adam hesitated, but carefully repeated his instructions, then said, "Sounds like you've thought of almost everything. But why don't you just put him on a bus? We could pick him up in Omaha."

"You don't know Harley. He'd go nuts on a bus all by himself. He's a goddamned window-lickin' idiot and helpless as hell around strangers. Plus, tellin' him he's goin' one way and I'm goin' another would cause a shitstorm you don't want to be responsible for."

Adam hesitated. He shifted the phone to his other ear. He stood. "Rufus let's get one thing straight. Nothing I could do would make me responsible for any of this. It is all on you, my friend, every degenerate bit of it."

"Well, now, the noxious weed man has a backbone."

"Backbone's fine. My stomach's the problem. Always churns a little when I smell a Piker."

"You still pissed about that ditch we put you in, ain't you? You better save all that for later, Thompson. Now, you goin' to help me get Harley home or not?"

Adam cooled. His angry exchange with Rufus was a mistake that felt good. He recovered quickly. "Rufus, I think I can help. First, I'd like to talk to a couple of people and call you back. How's that sound?"

"Damn it, Thompson, just make it happen. I don't have time for more people and more phone calls. You done things right for that Tedrow kid. Ricky, too, I guess. Now, do things right for Harley. I gotta catch a bus. Rufus hung up the phone, checked the coin slot for change, and inspected the queue of travelers at the ticket window, which was fifteen people long.

He spotted two likely candidates. One was a disheveled young man carrying his belongings in a garbage bag. The other was an older woman with a cane. He chose the young man because he was closer to the end of the line and because he was younger—a younger person would be less suspicious, Rufus thought. He approached the young man, put a hand on his shoulder, and said, "Hi, how you doin'? I got a ticket to Denver that I can't use. Would you like to have it?"

"Sure," the young man said. "How come?"

"Plans changed. Don't have time to mess with it. Yours if you want it."

"Thanks, man."

Knowing that the headcount on the bus would match the number of tickets sold, Rufus started his red pickup and headed for Billings, Montana. He hoped his pursuers would chase him to Denver.

15

Room 222

ADAM CALLED HUBERT ST. John immediately. "Hubert, you sittin' down?"

"Yep," Hubert answered. "Whatcha got?"

"Rufus Hudson just called me. He wants to give up Harley. Seems he's not cut out to be a fugitive. He's in Rapid City, South Dakota."

"Damn, Adam. You can't shake these guys, can you? Get up here right away. I'll call Salisbury."

"We're going to have to stop meeting like this, guys," Jason said, as he joined the other two men in Hubert's office. He sat beside Adam and looked across the desk at Hubert.

"Welcome, Jason. This is one meeting you'll be glad you attended," Hubert said. "Adam's new best friend, Rufus Hudson, called this morning. Please, talk to us Adam."

Adam wasted no time. He gave them the bottom line first. "Rufus wants to give up Harley," he said. "He's in Rapid City, South Dakota." Then he explained the call and the detailed instructions Rufus had given him. Jason and Hubert exchanged glances and sat quietly for several seconds after Adam finished speaking.

Finally, Jason spoke, "Adam, what is it about you? You are a Hudson brother magnet"

"That's not much to brag about," Adam said. "What's next?"

"There is no question, we must respond," Jason said. "Of course, Rufus could be sending us on a wild goose chase just to keep us occupied, but I doubt it. I don't think he'd pop his head out of the foxhole this far if he wasn't serious. First, we'll contact the authorities in Rapid City. They'll go get Harley, and then we'll figure out how to get him back here. Plus, somebody's got to take a hard look at the bus station to see if we can track Rufus, though I'll bet it's a dodge. Rufus is no dummy. Why would he tell us he was going to catch a bus, if that was his plan?"

"What time did he call?"

"About 8:30 this morning. Woulda been 7:30 in Rapid City."

"I'll contact Grey Hound in Rapid City to check destinations of buses leaving about then. We'll have someone there to meet the bus if the destination seems clear. I've got to put things in motion." Jason said, as he stood. "Thanks, Adam. You're the man."

"You will remind the guys who pick up Harley of his handicap, won't you?" Adam asked.

"Absolutely."

"Do you think they'll use the Abe Lincoln code?"

"That'll be up to them. I'll keep you posted," Jason said on his way out the door.

~~~~~~~~

About four hours later, two state troopers and a Rapid City–based sheriff stood at the Motel 6 check-in counter. The sheriff took the lead. "Hello, I'm County Sheriff Fowler," he said as he flashed his badge. This is State Trooper Magnusson and State Trooper Hooper." The troopers touched the brim of their hats. "We need to visit with one of your guests. He's in room 222. His name is Harley Hudson."

"Let me see. Rufus Smith has that room. Does that sound right?" asked the young, nervous female receptionist.

"That would be right. Harley expects us. But just in case he's not there, can you give us a key so we can wait for him."

The receptionist paused, eyeballed the three official-looking men, and said, "I'm supposed to go up with you and let you in.

But, I'm alone because Susan's late. I can't leave the desk, so that'd be okay. But, please return the key. She handed them a key to room 222 and immediately picked up the phone.

Sheriff Fowler tensed instinctively. "Please, don't call the room."

"Oh, no, sir. I understand. I was just checking on Susan."

"Good. Thank you."

"Hooper, you take the stairs, so that we can get a lay of the land. We'll take the elevator," Sheriff Fowler said. Hooper arrived at the second floor first. The elevator was incredibly slow. They stood in the short hallway just around the corner from the ice machine and room 222.

"When we leave, we are taking the stairs," Sheriff Fowler said.

"Okay. Time for a reality check," said Trooper Magnusson. "Are we really going to use that stupid Abraham Lincoln, double-knock code to get this guy. Why not just open the door and grab him? He's a kidnapper, for Christ's sake! I don't mind if we scare him a little."

"It's true. The code is comic book silly. Still, combined with what we know for sure, it may be the best bet. The guy's a simpleton. He could freeze or go bananas. We don't know which. If we use the key and take him by storm, he'll be surprised. But if we use the code, he may open the door with his guard down and be easier to contain. Plus, we'll be closer to him so we can grab him before he tries to jump through the plate glass window or lock himself in the bathroom. If we need to be aggressive, we will. But, let's try the code and a gentle approach based on the truth. His brother asked us to come get him and take him home."

The troopers stood to the left of the door, Sheriff Fowler to the right. "I'll do the knocking. Stand away from the door until it opens just in case he responds with something nasty. Unlikely, but better safe than sorry."

Sheriff Fowler knocked twice. Harley stirred but didn't fully awaken. Sheriff Fowler knocked twice a second time. Harley awoke. He thought he heard a double knock but was unsure. He got off the bed and walked near the door. Fowler held up a finger, indicating that he would knock twice one last time. Before he could do so, Harley answered uneasily, "Who's there?"

It was barely audible, but they heard it. Fowler answered, "Abraham Lincoln." Harley smiled and swung the door wide open. His face went blank as he stared at the three unfamiliar men standing before him.

"Harley, Rufus sent us to get you. He wants us to take you home," Sheriff Fowler said as he brushed past Harley to enter the room. The troopers followed, forcing Haley to take steps backward toward the bed.

"Where's Rufus?" Harley asked. "Where's Rufus?" he repeated.

"We don't know for sure. He's tied up doing something. He called us and asked us to help you get home."

"To see Ricky?" Harley asked.

"Ricky's your other brother, isn't he?"

"Yes."

"Rufus said Ricky will be glad to see you. Why don't you pack up your stuff, use the bathroom if you need to, and we can be on our way?"

The four men left the motel without incident. Harley was still confused about the absence of Rufus, but the promise of seeing Ricky seemed to soothe him. They placed him, handcuffed, in the back seat of the cruiser. Sheriff Fowler felt bad about cuffing him, since he had been so cooperative. Still, he was an unknown quantity and protocol demanded it. The sheriff joined him in the back seat. He assured Harley that he would see Ricky very soon. The next day, Deputy Hargrove met the South Dakota troopers at the halfway point and drove Harley to Spring Valley.

The bus ride from Rapid City to Denver took eight hours. It left at 8:15 a.m., shortly after Rufus called Adam. There was no other bus until noon, so they assumed the Denver bus was the Rufus bus. They knew it was a long shot. Still, two Denver detectives were there to meet the Greyhound motor coach as it pulled into the station. All passengers were accounted for, but Rufus was not among them.

16

Reinventing Snyder

RUFUS ENJOYED THE FIVE-HOUR drive to Billings, Montana. As he made his gradual descent into the Yellowstone Valley, the city lay before him and alluring mountain ranges surrounded him. He was optimistic, free and alone. He cherished his freedom. His solitude was welcome, but would become a heaviness he didn't understand.

He pulled off the freeway on the outskirts of the city to buy gas and stretch his legs. As he filled his tank, he spotted a used car lot a short distance away. Moments later his Toyota pickup was parked on the street alongside a lackluster assortment of used cars. Acquiring a new vehicle seemed necessary, but without the title it would be difficult. He had several choices. He could contact the Frederick County DMV, which would reveal his location. Stealing a car was an option, but driving a stolen vehicle could easily cause more problems than it solved. He could take his chances with the red Toyota pickup. Or, he could find a car dealer who was as corrupt as he was.

Coyote's Saloon sat directly across the street from where he parked. He chose to visit the saloon rather than the car lot. It was an out-west working man's bar with all the amenities—pool table, dartboard, and a pinball machine. He sat at the bar, ordered a beer, and turned toward the pool table to watch a spirited game of eight ball between two young cowboys. Shots made and shots missed caused howls, hoots, and laughter. The players' half-drunk buddies added to the racket. Rufus's first beer went down smoothly. He ordered another and then another, and almost forgot he was a fugitive.

The noise made him angry. Anger was what made Rufus tick. In his hometown it was his currency. The trouble was, he couldn't spend it in Billings, Montana. If he wanted to quiet pool players in Snyder, Nebraska, he'd simply slash the felt covering on the pool table. His intimidating dominance did not exist in Billings. The mean-spirited joy he usually found in his anger was gone. He left Coyote's Saloon, got in his red pickup, and stared down the road before him. It was a blocks-long clutter of fast-food cafes, gas stations, motels, and stop lights. Billings, Montana, was too big. He didn't know it yet, but reinventing Snyder would become his unspoken goal. He drove north on U.S. 87 to find a smaller hiding place.

He stopped in Stampede, about fifty miles north of Billings. He liked the looks of the town. It was not as small as Snyder, but it had personality. The sign outside the town read Welcome to Stampede. We cater to Cowpokes! It had some newer businesses, like Casey's convenience store and a Farmer's Supply store. They stood, conspicuous in their newness, across the street from a row of older downtown buildings. A small grocery store, the Saddle-Up Cafe, the Stampede Tavern, a real estate office, and a cowboy clothing store greeted Rufus as he maintained the twenty-five-miles-per-hour speed limit on Main Street. Three nearly vacant motels, a granary, a sale barn, and a rodeo arena were located at the north end of town.

He rented a room at the Bronc Buster Motel for two nights and backtracked to the restaurant for a hamburger and fries. After dark, he replaced the South Dakota plates with his Nebraska plates so his vehicle would be consistent with his driver's license. Tomorrow he would find a way to buy a different car.

17

Fishing for Corruption

HARLEY WAS SAFELY DELIVERED to the Frederick County jail in Spring Valley. They allowed him to visit with Ricky in a brightly lit common area with no windows. They were glad to see one another, although it was a worrisome reunion. The stress of the chase was over for them, but sitting at a table in a large common area, wearing orange jailhouse jumpsuits was not something either of them enjoyed.

"How long we gonna have to be in jail, Ricky?" Harley asked.

"I wish I knew, Harley," Ricky answered.

"Maybe Rufus will come get us."

"No, Harley. That ain't goin' to happen."

"This all 'cause we took that kid?"

"We didn't take the kid. Rufus did. We was just there when he did it. Can you remember that? It's important. Tell me what I just said."

"We didn't take the kid. Rufus did. We was just there when he did it," Harley repeated.

Ricky reached across the table and patted Harley's arm. "Good. That's perfect. If anybody asks you about takin' that Tedrow boy, that's what you say to 'em. Nothing more."

Harley pushed his chair back and brought his foot, heel first, to the top of the table. "Do you like my new shoes?" Harley asked.

"I noticed them. Those are nice. Where'd you get 'em?"

"Rufus got 'em for me," Harley said, as he swung his foot down. "Got me a new shirt too. When we went to see the presidents."

"The what?"

"You know, them presidents that's carved on that mountain."

"You mean Mount Rushmore. Rufus took you there?"

"Yeah. It was fun. Next day I had my second big ol' whipped-cream waffle. Then he took me to the motel and told me to stay there while he got us a new car. Next thing I knowed, cops was there. They said Rufus told them to come get me and bring me to see you. Why do think he done that, Ricky? I don't like jail."

"Rufus did you a favor, Harley. He did you a big favor. We'll be okay."

~~~~~~

Rufus wasn't in jail, but he was held captive by intractable bad habits. He didn't miss his brothers. He missed controlling them. Rufus needed someone and someplace to dominate. He hoped Stampede was the answer. Breakfast and a hot cup of coffee would be an excellent place to begin.

"Cakes and bacon's the special this morning—only three fifty. Fifty cents more for coffee," said the young, but hard-looking, waitress. Her name tag read Patty.

"Sounds good," Rufus answered. "You live around here, Patty?"

"Twenty miles up the road," she answered. "You take cream?"

"Yes. Where would a guy buy a car around here?"

"Want something new, you'll have to go down to Billings. There's a used car lot up in Buffalo. That's where I live. Be careful what you buy from Old Turtle Head, though. Most of his cars have seen better days. He calls them pre-owned. We call them pre-scrapyard."

"Turtle Head?"

"That's what we call him because he looks like a turtle. Ain't got no neck. Looks like he's peeking out from under a shell at ya."

"Alright, I'll go see Old Turtle Head. Don't guess that's what I oughta call him, though."

Rufus and the Weed Man

"No. His name's Reginald Higgins. Goes by Reggie. Let me get your order in before you starve," Patty said. As she walked away from Rufus's table, she turned and greeted a new and familiar customer in a state trooper uniform. "Hey, Dwight. How ya doin'? Been catching any criminals?" He shifted his gun belt to sit comforably at the counter.

"I haven't had breakfast yet. Can't catch criminals until ya have breakfast, can ya? Coffee, orange juice, and buscuits and gravy please," Trooper Dwight responded.

Rufus was uneasy but unruffled. It would arouse suspicion if he left before he'd eaten. So, he sat. Patty delivered his coffee and a small plastic pitcher of cream.

"Thanks," Rufus said. He spotted a newspaper on a chair two tables away. "Okay, if I take a look at that," he asked, pointing to the paper.

"Oh, sure." Patty brought it to him. He hid behind it, reading until his breakfast came. He ate, paid his bill, left a trifling tip, walked undetected past the trooper, and was on his way to Buffalo to see Turtle Head Higgins.

He breathed easier as he drove away from the cafe, chuckling at his earlier nervousness. His breakfast with a state trooper was a nonevent, but it did underscore how worrisome situations can arise unexpectadly. He must be watchful if he wanted future brushes with the law to be as smooth as his first. It also reminded him that a successful fugitive life could only be his if he stayed out of trouble. Until now, Rufus hadn't thought past his next hamburger, but the Trooper's casual visit to the Saddle Up Cafe etched the 'first commandment' into his fugitive-survival checklist. He had to behave. He'd probably need to push his luck a little to solve his automobile problem. After that, he'd become a model citizen.

He pulled his pickup into the used car lot, parked by the trailer that served as the office, and walked the front line of used cars parked beneath the fluttering plastic pennants. A man with no hair, no neck, and a broad smile approached across the blacktopped lot. He wore a western shirt buttoned to the top and a bolo tie that seemed to grow out of his chin.

"Howdy. Lookin' to trade your Toyota pickup?" the man said. "Give you a deal on it. They are in high demand around here. My name's Reggie." He shook Rufus's hand. Rufus knew immediately why they called him Turtle Head.

"Name's Rufus. Don't know what I want to do. Just thought I'd look around a bit. What ya asking for that blue Jeep Cherokee over there?"

"You've got good taste. That's a sweetheart of a car. Only has ninety thousand actual on her. She's a steal for ninety-five hundred dollars."

"My trade bring it down to about three thousand, I suppose."

"Well, I don't know if we'll get there. Let me take a closer look at your car. I'll see what we can do." They walked over to Rufus's pickup, and Reggie went through the motions. "Nice truck. You've taken good care of her. Got Nebraska plates. You from Nebraska?"

"Yeah, used to be. Looking to find a place here. I'm a cattleman." Then he took a chance and went fishing for corruption. "Darned title is all the way down in Nebraska. I was hopin' not to have to call down there to get it. Don't have the time. Any way you can help me?"

Reggie stiffened. He raised his head above his collar as far as he could, looked over the top of his glasses, and said, "You askin' me to create a new title for you?"

"I didn't know you could do that. Can you? That would be great."

"I didn't say I could do it. I asked if that's what you want me to do."

"Well, I didn't mean to offend you. I just figured you was a good businessman."

The posturing was over. Rufus sold used houses. Reggie sold used cars. They both knew the code words. Being called a good businessman meant that Rufus was willing to pay.

"I don't know for sure, but I may be able to line somebody up to help you. Won't be cheap, though."

"How much?"

"Still want the Cherokee?"

"Let's separate 'em. How much for the new title for my pickup without a trade, a title that will let me get legal Montana plates."

"Well, that's a little different," Reggie said. He paused, fiddled with his bolo tie and snugged it up beneath his chin. "With a trade, I can make a little money on the Jeep, which would reduce the cost of the title. By itself, I couldn't make it happen for less than seven hundred dollars."

Rufus took a deep breath and exhaled slowly. "I'll give you five hundred. That's three hundred now, cash money. And the rest when I get the plates."

Reggie grimaced as if someone had dropped a brick on his foot. Then shook his head. "No way. Sorry. I can't do that."

"Okay, six hundred. And that's it."

"That'll work only if you pay for the whole thing up front."

"You are a good businessman, aren't you?" Rufus hated to spend so much cash in one spot so soon but knew finding another Turtlehead Higgins would be difficult, maybe impossible. He considered the expense a prudent investment in his future and said, "Deal."

"It'll take a day to put it together. You got a local mailing address?"

"Not yet. Stayin' in Stampede."

"Get one. P.O. box will do. Post office is in the grocery store down at Stampede if that's where you want to be. There's an actual post office in Buffalo. Buffalo may suit you better. Plus, my cousin's got some apartments there if you want to take a look."

"No. I ain't ready to pick a place just yet. I'll run down to Stampede. When and where do I get my plates?"

"You'll have to come back up here first. Get your P.O. box, then come see me. We can complete a little paper work, and you can go up to the vehicle registration office in downtown Buffalo. You gotta wait a day, now. I won't have things set up until the day after tomorrow. When you go up there, make sure you go to Gene Rinker's window. He's a big guy with wavy, blond hair and a pock-marked face. Usually on window three. Go to him. Give him the paperwork. He'll take care of you."

Reggie started to walk away, then turned and slapped his palm on the pickup hood. "Don't go to anyone else. If Gene ain't there, leave and go back later. You gotta work with Gene."

"Got it," Rufus said.

Two days later, Rufus was sporting Montana plates and driving legal. The truck was registered to Jerome Rufus Hudson, which was his given name. He would go by J.R. Hudson in his new community. Turtlehead Higgins didn't lie. Red pickups were popular vehicles in Montana. With legal plates, his truck was a good place to hide. Besides, he liked his pickup better than the Jeep.

18

The Trial

"Are you ready for the Hudson boys, Jason?" Hubert asked. The two men sat in the prosecutor's office the day before the Hudson brother trial. Salisbury was calm. St. John sat in the guest chair, resting his thumbs behind his suspenders. "Are you ready. Do you have your ducks in a row?" he said.

"Yeah, it should be pretty cut and dried," Jason answered.

"You going to push for punishment or leniency?"

"Well, they were there when Jimmy was taken. They held him captive, though they probably did it under duress. Especially Ricky. He's the one who helped us find Jimmy and bring him home. Of course, Harley was born to be a follower. If we only had Rufus, it would be simpler to go easy on them," Jason answered.

"Easier? What do you mean, easier?" Hubert said.

"Kidnapping is an emotional crime. People want someone to pay. We know that Rufus is the evil one, the one responsible for the deed. If we had him to prosecute, we could give him both barrels and let the other two off with a slap on the wrist. Without him, the other two will pay a higher price just because people expect it."

"Do the courts care about what the people expect?"

"They shouldn't, but they do."

"You sound like a politician. You running for governor or looking for justice?"

Jason was silent. He stood, walked to the window, raised the shade, and looked down at the flawless courthouse lawn, clicked his ballpoint pen twice, and returned to his chair. "I know. You're right. And I'm glad you called me on it."

"It's not every day you get a high-profile kidnapping case to prosecute. You're forgiven."

The two men had hardly known each other before the Tedrow kidnapping. Now, they were friends who spoke freely to one another. Hubert admired Jason's energy and intellect, but he was often troubled by his opportunistic ambition. Hubert's age and experience, reinforced by his quirky suspenders and bow tie, brought clarity to the conversation.

"Well, the trial starts tomorrow. It'll be out of our hands very soon," Jason said.

"Adam Thompson going to testify?"

"Yes. He's first up" answered Jason.

"Now, there's one solid citizen," Hubert said.

"Indeed."

~~~~~~

Scott called his dad the night before the trial. Adam tried to seem unconcerned about testifying, but he couldn't hide his nervousness.

"Tomorrow's a big day, isn't it? Who knew a simple trip to Snyder would turn into such a never-ending ordeal? You'll do fine, Dad. You'll do fine," Scott said.

"Yes, I suppose. No reason to be nervous about tellin' the truth," Adam said. "I will admit sittin' in a courtroom will be new territory for me. Has been quite a ride, hasn't it?"

Almost two months had passed since Adam first met the Hudson brothers. His day-to-day routine had returned to normal, although he had new respect for the social diversities of Frederick County. Plus, he was no longer surprised when people identified him as the guy who saved the kidnapped kid. He didn't like it and hoped the special attention would pass in time. Both Mike and Scott inadvertently added to his celebrity. They were proud of him and told his story often, with emphasis on how such an unassuming, regular guy could become such an essential part of the Frederick County crime of the decade.

The Omaha attorney who usually defended the Hudson brothers was a longtime Rufus connection. Ricky chose not to use him. Stephen Simmons, the court-appointed attorney was young and smart but led by curiosity at times rather than courtroom wisdom.

The jury was composed of six men, six women, and one alternate male juror who would hear all of the evidence but not participate in jury deliberation unless needed. None of the jurors lived in Snyder, Nebraska. Defense Attorney Simmons had seen to that after he learned of the community hatred toward the Hudson brothers. In the minds of most Snyder folks, the Hudson brothers were a single, fearsome threat. Keith and Becky Tedrow were among the handful of people who could distinguish one brother from the other. They attended the trial. So did Jimmy, who would also testify.

Adam was nervous when he took the stand. Then he looked out across the gallery, saw Jimmy sitting there with his parents, and became calm and determined.

"I understand that you were involved in Jimmy Tedrow's release from captivity. Is that correct?" Simmons asked.

Adam said, "Yes, accidentally. But, yes, I participated."

"What do you mean by accidentally?" Simmons knew he had to handle Adam with kid gloves. On the one hand, he wanted to reveal Ricky's note on Adam's back window. On the other, he wanted to avoid any reference to the cattle guard ambush, which made the Hudsons look like a team of cold-hearted ruffians.

"I visited the Hudson place as a part of my job." He explained his job as the noxious weed supervisor of Frederick County. "While I was there, someone wrote a note in the dust on the back window of my pickup. It read 'The Barn.' That note, combined with a phone call to the sheriff, led us to the Hudsons and Jimmy's return home."

"Who wrote the note."

"Sheriff Bartlow told me Ricky's prints were in the dust. Which would make sense, because Ricky was outside the house while I visited with his brothers inside. It was his tip to us that Jimmy was being held in their barn."

The young attorney deviated from his pretrial playbook. "So, how did you connect the dots? How did you know a vague note like 'The Barn' was connected to Jimmy Tedrow's kidnapping?"

"We didn't until I met with the county attorney to discuss how to deal with the injuries I received during a reckless trick they pulled on me that day."

So, there it was. All the jury-selection caution that Simmons had used to avoid showing the brothers as a trouble-making threesome was for naught. He knew Jason Salisbury would exploit the opportunity now that the door was open, so he tried to turn his error into an advantage. Adam had to become an unworthy witness because of his deep-seated bias due to the Hudson dirty trick.

"Reckless trick. What sort of trick did they pull on you?" Simmons asked.

He told them the story of the cattle-guard ambush. Then Simmons asked another question out of sheer curiosity.

"You mean to tell me that the Hudson brothers had Jimmy Tedrow held captive in their barn and decided to prank a government employee who just happened into their yard that day? Why would they take such a chance?"

"Seemed like a foolish attempt to be entertained to me. But I really don't know."

"Did you press charges."

"No. Jimmy Tedrow's problem came up at the same time. It just seemed more important to find Jimmy than to punish someone for the bump on my head."

"So, you have never received any legal satisfaction for the pain and suffering they caused you."

"No."

"How do you feel about that? How angry are you?"

"I'm not angry at the Hudson brothers. I'm angry at Rufus. The harder I look, the tougher it is to stuff them all in the same basket. They are three different people, each with a different reason for being where they are today."

"Why were you involved in the Tedrow case? What does kidnapping have to do with noxious weeds?"

"Blame that on my business cards. When I visited them, I gave them business cards as I left. They had my number, so they called me. I became a go-between for the Hudsons and the authorities. When they wanted to release Jimmy, they contacted me. I don't know why. When Rufus wanted to send Harley home from South Dakota, he called me. I don't know why. Maybe it was just convenient. Or, it might have been because I was a government man but not a lawman. Or, maybe they felt like they knew me because of my visit. I don't know, but it made sense to do as they asked, so I did."

While the young attorney needed to improve his cross-examination technique, he was proficient in courtroom theatrics. He walked to his table and spoke softly to his assistant, asking her to pretend to check her notepad and look up and nod her head. She did. He returned the nod and circled back to stand directly before the jury, with his hand on the jury-box rail. He faced the witness stand and revisited Adam's earlier answer with a slow and deliberate question. "So, your experience with the Hudsons tells you that each brother shares a different level of guilt in this matter?"

"Yes," Adam said. "Ricky was responsible for Jimmy's release. He made a phone call, wrote a message in the dust, sent me a letter with the release plan. Harley? Well, he's sorta slow. God gave him the ability to make little decisions, not big ones. That leaves Rufus. Seems to me, it was his impulsive temperament that started this problem and his stubbornness that kept it going."

"Objection!" Prosecutor Salisbury interrupted. He hated to blindside Adam, but courtroom decorum demanded it. "This witness is not a mental health expert and his assessment of Harley Hudson's mental capacity is not permissible. Nor is his opinion about Rufus Hudson. Neither are based on facts and they should be stricken."

The judge concurred. "Objection sustained. The jury will disregard the testimony in question."

Adam was surprised by Salisbury's objection, although he knew he was just doing his job. He also knew that the objection didn't alter the truth of what he said, and, at times, the truth is tough to disregard. He hoped this was one of those times.

Simmons's attempt to discredit Adam did just the opposite. Adam's testimony was the first verse in a chorus of vindicating support for Ricky and Harley. Jimmy Tedrow's testimony added to the refrain, as he explained Ricky's kindness during his captivity. Sheriff Bartlow explained Ricky's willingness to cooperate after the arrest. Simmons had taken the jury precisely where he wanted them to be, even though the route he took was indirect and unplanned. Salisbury let it happen. It was what he wanted too.

Harley didn't testify. Ricky did. Salisbury worked his way toward one difficult question. He asked if he had written the note, called the sheriff, and helped with the plan to release Jimmy. Ricky answered that he had.

"Why did you sneak up on it like that? Why not stop Rufus as soon as he grabbed Jimmy. You knew what he was doing was wrong. Why wait so long? Why didn't you act immediately?"

Ricky looked away from Salisbury's questioning eyes. He thought for a moment, looked straight at the prosecutor, and said, "I don't know. I never thought of doin' that. But, thinkin' about it now, I can tell you it woulda been a bad time to challenge Rufus."

"You mean because he'd been drinking?'

"Yeah, and because he was mad. When he gets mad, it ain't no fun."

Defense Attorney Simmons took his turn. "Rufus is quite a bit older than you, isn't he?"

"Twelve years."

"So, he was the head of the family after your father died. Is that right?

"Yes."

"Rufus sort of served as your dad, didn't he? I suppose doing as he asked was just the way of things. Right?"

"Yeah, I guess. Rufus was always in charge. No doubt about that. When he grabbed Jimmy, I felt deep-down bad. I said to let him go, but that just made Rufus mad. When he's mad, stayin' quiet is the only smart thing. Guess it took some time for me to see around Rufus. You know, to be sure my feelin's was right and to know what I was about to do was right. By that time, about all I could do was leave notes, make secret phone calls, and try to convince Rufus to let Jimmy go . . . real careful like."

Both brothers were charged with aiding and abetting a kidnapping. Jason Salisbury explained the letter of the law in his closing. "The law makes no provision for splitting hairs," he insisted. "Those who aid and abet are as guilty as the person who commits the crime."

The jury deliberated for only two hours. They were convinced of Rufus's guilt and his brother's involuntary participation in the kidnapping, but they couldn't forget that the crime occurred because the Hudsons were stealing tires from Emil Williams's car. They simply couldn't let them off scot-free.

During jury deliberation, the jury foreman, who was a retired schoolteacher, emphasized their shared guilt. "There's a reason for leniency here folks, but there's also a reason for punishment. Those boys participated. They are lawbreakers. Eventually, they did what was right, but they participated. They need to be punished." The jury found them guilty, but recommended leniency. Harley was sentenced to eighteen months in the state penitentiary with the possibility of parole after one year. Ricky was sentenced to one year with credit for time served. In six months, he would be free.

19

Rodeo Week

RUFUS MOVED OUT OF the Bronc Buster Motel a week after he got his Montana license plates. He'd found a part-time job at the Stampede Sale Barn and a permanent place to live on the same day. He was proud of himself. He had secured the necessities for survival, although his loneliness persisted. Now, he would work on easing his solitude.

Stampede was a rodeo town. In April, the junior rodeo circuit kicked off the season with a one-day event at the Stampede Arena. In June, the regional competition for the Montana Association of Rodeo Cowboys was in town for three days. They called it Rodeo Week. Then, in August there were two weekend training events for aspiring bull riders. Rufus learned about that cowboy summer when he tried to rent one of five trailer houses that sat near the arena.

"I noticed them trailer houses out there by the rodeo grounds. Wonder if a fella could rent one of 'em?" Rufus asked his boss. The stockyards and sale barn were just up the road from the rodeo arena.

"Them's cowboy cabins. Rodeo Board rents 'em out to cowboys when they come to town," his boss answered. His name was Buck Blankenship. He was a lean, friendly man with a tanned face weathered beyond its years, a man born to wear Levi's and cowboy boots. He hired J.R. Hudson to help move livestock at the sale barn during the weekly auctions. Rufus earned twelve dollars cash for each day he worked. He called it macaroni money. He wasn't working for the money as much as he was for a place to ease his loneliness.

The Stampede Sale Barn sold sheep on Wednesdays, hogs on Thursdays, and cattle on Fridays. Rufus had a place to go three days a week, and he found a friend. He worked closely with Buck's nephew, Bobby, as they moved one lot of livestock after another into the auction arena to be sold by the chattering auctioneer. They also cleaned out the holding pens at day's end. Rufus didn't mind. He enjoyed talking to Bobby. Rufus called him a deep thinker.

"What about between now and then? The trailers just sit empty?" Rufus asked.

"Don't know. Never seen 'em rented, except to cowboys during rodeo events. You'd have to talk to Albert Bennett about that. He's chairman of the Rodeo Board, and he owns the sale barn. "He's comin' by today. I'll have him talk with ya."

The impromptu meeting between Albert Bennett and Rufus was productive even though the cowboy trailers were not for rent. Their water and power were off, and Albert was unwilling to turn them on until April. "Besides, I don't think you'd want to live in one of 'em. Cowboys trash 'em terrible," Albert said. "But I do have a furnished one-bedroom cottage near downtown that might work for you. Want to check it out?"

The next day Rufus inspected the little house and rented it on the spot. It was an old single-story bungalow cloaked in a fresh coat of white paint. A huge elm tree buckled the aging sidewalk that led to the house. The fresh paint couldn't hide the stable, but sagging, porch roof. It was in one of Stampede's oldest neighborhoods, just up the hill from the business district and the Stampede Tavern. It was modestly furnished but had everything he needed, even a TV. Putting down one month's rent for a security deposit, plus rent for the month reminded him that he might have to sneak back to Snyder to get more cash sometime soon. His new home's proximity to the tavern and his misguided affection for Bobby helped hasten the need for such a trip.

J.R. Hudson lived quietly in his freshly painted cottage and worked three or four days a week at the sale barn for a little more than eight months. At first, Buck thought Rufus was a godsend because of how he took to Bobby. Rufus bought him pop and snacks and seldom let Bobby out of his sight as they worked. He even devised a manure-scooping game on cattle days to entertain Bobby. Each man occupied an empty, soiled holding pen. Rufus yelled, 'Go!' and the manure-scooping race began. They ran the full length of the slippery, forty-foot pen with the scoop shovel skidding on the manure-covered concrete before them. They emptied their full shovels into wheelbarrows and returned for another pass. It took at least fifteen trips to cover the entire pen. Bobby usually won and was totally entertained. Rufus's loneliness was eased. Buck appreciated the shortened cleanup times. However, he was slightly troubled by the possessiveness that had seeped into J.R.'s relationship with his nephew.

As Rodeo Week competition neared, Stampede came to life. Cowboys, cowgirls, and gawking tourists started to appear days before the three-day event, which was scheduled for the end of June. The motels and the cowboy cabins were full, and the Stampede Tavern was the center of activity. Even though it was just two blocks from his cottage, Rufus had been there only once. He remembered how difficult it had been to hold his temper after three beers and a noisy pool game in the Billings tavern. He could not allow that to happen again. Staying home, having a beer with supper, and turning in after watching TV became a comfortable routine. It had been months since he had unleashed a volley of angry curse words at someone or had become belligerent and destructive just for the fun of it. His changed behavior, however, didn't reveal a reformed heart. It was simply a masquerade that kept him free.

The sale barn was closed during the rodeo merriment, and Buck gave him a ticket to the championship competition on Friday, which included performances by the best bull riders and bronc busters in Montana. Having never attended a live rodeo, Rufus looked forward to the event with almost childlike anticipation. Rodeo Week was one long, reverberating party, a party easily heard from Rufus's cottage. Raucous swells of laughter, shouts, loud music, and louder mufflers drifted up the hill as Rufus prepared his supper with an eye on the television weatherman. When a party consumes an entire community, it is difficult not to participate. Rufus finished his mac and cheese and yielded to his curiosity. He turned off the TV and walked down the hill to the Stampede Tavern.

The place was packed. The tavern was longer than it was wide, making the space seem like a giant, elongated boxcar full of cowboys, cowgirls, and buxom waitresses delivering beer. Cowboy hats bobbed, spun, and hovered, taking up more space than necessary. Rufus found an uncomfortable place to sit on the protruding sill of the plate glass window in the front of the tavern. A perky waitress in a puffy peasant blouse brought him a beer. He gave her one dollar, and she gave him a disappointed smile and moved on.

The pool table sat toward the rear of the room. Rufus saw Buck shooting pool and Bobby seated on a stool alongside the cue rack, sipping a soft drink. The room was simply too crowded to join them. He waved, but they didn't see him. The puffy-bloused waitress brought him another beer and retrieved his empty glass. The second beer went down easy.

Rufus wore clean overalls, his Walmart shirt, and his manure-stained boots. With no hat, he was underdressed, but he didn't know it. He stood and squeezed his considerable girth through the crowd toward an empty stool at the bar. He reached the open seat just before a young woman, also hoping to sit, reached the stool. He smiled at her and sat down and turned to the bartender and ordered another draft. He drank three more and hit a cognitive brick wall. On the outside, he looked like a slightly inebriated, middle-aged, overweight man. On the inside, he was a tangle of disturbing, emotional confusion.

He was closer to Buck and Bobby now, although there was still a crush of celebrating cowboy hats between him and his friends. He got off the stool and screamed, "Hey, Harley, let's go see the presidents! Harley, goddamn it, let's go home."

People heard his voice but not his words. There was too much noise. Buck and Bobby were only vaguely aware of some momentary disturbance across the room. Rufus would not be denied. He pushed his way through the crowd screaming, "Harley, let's go see the presidents!"

The crowd opened for the stumbling, drunken man and then closed behind him. Rufus stood directly in front of Bobby, screaming. His confusion had turned to full-throated anger. "Harley, we gotta go home. Get your idiot ass off that stool. We gotta go now!"

Bobby just stared. Buck laid his pool cue across the table and moved between Rufus and his nephew. He placed his hand on Rufus's shoulder to try and calm him. Rufus pushed his hand away and moved close enough to Bobby to grab his arm and pull him off the stool. Rufus gripped Bobby's arm and stood nose to nose with him, bellowing, "Harley, move your idiot ass. Do what I tell you. Get in the fuckin' truck and right now! You deep-thinkin' retard. Goddamn it, move!"

Buck had no choice. He grabbed Rufus's arm and spun him so they faced one another. He grasped the Walmart shirt with his left hand and pulled Rufus toward him in a violent, purposeful jerk. At the same time, he thrust his right fist forward, landing a single, powerful punch squarely on the bridge of Rufus's nose. Buck felt Rufus go limp and released him. Rufus dropped slowly to the floor into a seated position. There he sat, stunned and bleeding.

Buck nodded at his pool-game partner, who came to assist. They pulled Rufus to his feet. Each took an arm and walked the stumbling man through the crowd and into the street. They propped him up against the building's brick wall so they could catch their breath.

"Who is this guy? Do you know him?" Buck's friend asked.

"Yeah, he works for me. Been a good guy, up till now. I have no idea what got into the crazy sumbitch." Rufus leaned against the wall, unbalanced and with only a foggy awareness of where he was and what he had done.

"Look. I know where he lives. It's just up the hill. Go back and keep an eye on Bobby. I'll walk him home and deal with this tomorrow."

Buck's friend returned to the tavern. Its celebrating patrons resumed their revelry as if nothing had happened. The Rufus scuffle was just one of several altercations that would occur at the Stampede Tavern during Rodeo Week. One punch could hardly be considered a bar fight. There was no reason to call the police.

Rufus awoke with a pounding headache. He shuffled to the bathroom, looked in the mirror at his broken nose, swollen face, and the dried blood in his whiskers and knew his stay in Stampede was over.

During nearly eight months in Stampede, J.R. Hudson had made few friends. Bobby was a friend. Buck was friendly, but not a friend. Patty, the waitress at the Saddle-Up Cafe, knew him by name. He drove up to Buffalo several times to chat with Turtle Head Higgins because he felt they were kindred spirits. Higgins finally asked him to stop dropping by. It wasn't because he disliked Rufus, but they'd been partners in crime, and he felt a social relationship was unwise. Most of the regulars at the sale barn knew "J.R." just as part of the sale barn crew. He was known, but not known well. He'd led an exemplary fugitive life, and he was proud of his deceptiveness. Still, a persistent emptiness lingered. It was time to go home. He packed and tossed the cottage key on the kitchen table. Sticking around long enough to collect his rental deposit would be unwise, and he was glad to be headed for Snyder, Nebraska.

20

Cash Cache

ADAM BRAGGED ABOUT KEITH Tedrow. He thought the depth of his gratitude to Ricky Hudson was extraordinary. Those who didn't know the whole story thought it was a perfect example of the power of forgiveness. Keith would have argued the point. In his mind, Ricky's actions demanded applause, not forgiveness.

Keith asked to meet with Ricky two days before he was released from prison. He wanted to say thanks. As things turned out, he did much more. Keith took Ricky home on the day of his release, made the down payment on an old Honda Civic, and co-signed the financing agreement. He helped make things livable at the Hudson farmhouse. He made sure utilities, including the phone, were reconnected. Keith said it was the least he could do.

Sometimes lifelong bonds don't take much glue. The spontaneous kindness that allowed one cutting board to receive two grades came from the same heart that made the down payment on Ricky's car thirty years later. Adam wished Rufus had been exposed to the same lovely contagion sometime along his way.

Ricky had been out of prison for about two months, and it was a time of change. He had a car. He was working second shift at the chicken processing plant in Eddyville, and he found thousands of dollars hidden in a secret cavity beneath the refrigerator. He and Keith wouldn't have found it if it hadn't been for the foul smell that greeted them when they came in the back door on Ricky's first day home. It was not overwhelming, just a constant dull stench, which open windows wouldn't eliminate. They found brittle remains of the oozy-eyed cat near the back door and disposed of it, but the odor remained. Then they opened the refrigerator. The meat in the freezer had thawed, liquified, and seeped throughout the fridge in a fetid, sticky coating of decomposition. A replacement fridge was necessary. The next day, when Keith maneuvered a used refrigerator into place, he accidentally dislodged a two-foot, rectangular slab of linoleum-covered floorboard. It popped up to reveal a secret recess beneath the floor and an ammunition box full of cash.

They found forty-five thousand dollars in one-hundred-dollar bills, packaged in bundles of fifty, inside the box. It was more money than either man had ever seen in one place. They were dumbfounded, especially Keith, who had a better appreciation of the value of money than Ricky. Whatever money Ricky had, had been doled out to him by Rufus.

"What in the world, Ricky? Whose money is this?"

"I don't know. It must be Rufus's."

"Where would he get this kind of money?"

"I don't know. Sometimes guys would come by once in a while, and they'd talk about selling houses and stuff. But he told me and Harley that it was his business and we should stay out of it," Ricky answered. "What should we do with it?"

"We need to be careful here, Ricky. This much money can turn good luck into bad luck real fast. It must be Rufus's money. That means it isn't your money, so you'd better not spend it. Whosever it is, it should be stored in a safer place than this. Why don't we put it in a safety deposit box over at the Farmer's State Bank in Eddyville until we can talk to someone about what to do with it."

"A what box?"

"Safety deposit box. It's a place at a bank where you can keep valuable stuff."

"Okay, will you go with me?"

"Sure. Let's go right now. That much money sittin' around makes me nervous."

Keith and Ricky rented a safety deposit box. They paid with a one-hundred-dollar bill off the top stack of Rufus's money. The fee was ten dollars annually. Keith put the change in the bank box on top of the other neatly stacked bills. Ricky took a fifty-dollar bill from the loose change and asked, "How much that refrigerator cost you?"

"Forty bucks," Keith answered.

"Here. Take this. I owe you all that and a lot more," and pressed it into Keith's palm.

"But, Ricky, we don't know if the money is yours to spend."

"Don't care. Please take it," Ricky said. Keith took it, folded it, and tucked it in an out-of-sight corner of his wallet. Eventually, he would spend it without reluctance, but not soon. Ricky kept the key to the safety deposit box on a chain around his neck.

2 1

Unfamiliar Freedom

RUFUS'S HEAD ACHED AND he had only a jumbled recollection of his night at the Stampede Tavern. He remembered the bar, the beer, and the bobbing cowboy hats. He also had a quick-flash memory of seeing Harley, which made no sense at all. The only thing that made sense was to keep moving. Whatever flying object had smashed into his face would surely come back to haunt him. He stopped at Casey's to buy gas, Tylenol, coffee, and a glazed donut and began his two-day trip back to Snyder, Nebraska.

Even in his bruised, hungover condition, his survival instincts remained strong. Leaving Stampede was imperative. He needed money, so a clandestine trip to Snyder was his best option. He hadn't decided whether he would just slip in and take just enough money to get by for a while or take the whole stash. He'd decide when he got there. Rufus headed back toward Billings breathing through his mouth but with renewed self-assurance. His stay in Stampede had proven that survival as a fugitive was possible.

His license plates were legal, and he drove the speed limit. He didn't have the energy to chart a course on back roads, so he crossed South Dakota on I-90 and dropped down through Pike County on Highway 72. By eight o'clock the next evening, he was an hour out of Snyder. He stopped at a truck stop and enjoyed a leisurely cup of coffee and a slice of apple pie. He wanted to be sure that he arrived home after dark.

It was nearly ten o'clock when he slowed his pickup to a near stop in front of the mailbox mounted on the wrought iron letter H. He shut off his headlights and turned into the lane to his farmhouse, which the moonlight silhouetted in the distance. He drove slowly up the lane and over the cattle guard, which no longer rattled because it was properly anchored in a bed of concrete. He didn't notice the change. What he noticed was a surge of comfortable familiarity. After over 200 days on the run, he was home. His house, his barn, and his money were where they should be, and so was he. He steered wide to the right as he approached the house to avoid the noisy gravel.

Perhaps the house was abandoned, or maybe someone was there sleeping. He didn't know. He had no knowledge of his brothers' imprisonment and was sure of only one thing: There was plenty of money beneath the refrigerator. He parked out of sight on the far side of the barn. Flashlight in hand, he entered the house through the unlocked back door. He aimed the flashlight at the floor so that a light beam didn't streak through the window. He walked through the kitchen to inspect the living room and the adjoining bedroom, where he found an unmade bed. He ascended the creaky stairs to the second floor half expecting someone to stir and turn on a light. No one did. Both upstairs bedrooms were dark and unused.

When he returned to the kitchen, he turned on the light and found other signs of life. A dry dishcloth was draped across the edge of the sink. An opened bag of chips and two fresh apples sat on the countertop. Plus, there was a new refrigerator.

~~~~~~

The second shift at the chicken plant began at three thirty in the afternoon and lasted until eleven o'clock. Ricky was usually home by eleven thirty. This day would be no different.

He entered darkened house through the back door, turned on the kitchen light, and walked to the counter. He poured a small helping of chips into a cereal bowl. He circled the kitchen table and took one step toward the refrigerator and froze in his tracks.

The new fridge sat at an angle. Someone had walked its left side forward, exposing the now-open hiding place. The trap door and the empty ammunition box were tossed to the side. There was movement in the living room doorway.

"Hello, Ricky," Rufus said.

Ricky yelped and stumbled back toward the sink, bumping into the table as he did. He dodged behind the table, finding refuge between it and the sink. "You scared the hell out of me, Rufus. How long you been here?"

"That don't matter, Ricky. What matters is my money. Where the hell is it?" If Rufus had a trace of affection for his youngest brother, it was quickly eclipsed by his escalating rage. He became louder and more threatening with each step toward Ricky.

"Where the fuck is my money?" he screamed. He lunged and grasped at Ricky's shirt sleeve. Ricky sidestepped and moved away.

"In the bank. It's in the bank," Ricky shouted.

"The bank. What do you know about banks? You never been in one." Rufus snarled, as he moved toward Ricky's end of the small, oval table.

"Keith helped me with it." Ricky continued to circle the table, moving away from Rufus's angry, lumbering shuffle.

Rufus stopped. "Who the hell is Keith?"

"Keith Tedrow. Jimmy Tedrow's dad."

"You goddamned moron!" Rufus screamed. "Why did you show him my money?" Veins bulged in his temples as he tossed a chair toward the far end of the room and grabbed the edge of the table and flipped it on its side, thrusting his weight against the leg-side of the table, trying to pin Ricky against the wall with the tabletop.

Ricky eluded the table. He was younger, stronger, and faster than Rufus and did something that he had never done. He screamed at his domineering big brother, "You crazy, son of a bitch. Shut up and sit down!" He shot past the overturned table and ran straight toward Rufus in a targeted bull rush, which landed his shoulders in Rufus's chest. It sent Rufus skidding on his butt across the floor. "Shut up and sit down. Shut up and sit down," Ricky screamed as he hovered over his surprised and overmatched brother. He grabbed a kitchen chair and sat it down hard on the floor beside Rufus. He pushed the chair against the wall with his foot. "Shut up and sit down. Sit down right here, in this chair. Do it now!"

Rufus struggled to stand, but he did. Ricky backed Rufus toward the chair with a sequence of short, two-handed shoves to Rufus's chest, forcing him to sit. Ricky wasn't finished. He pushed the overturned table toward Rufus, legs first, trapping the seated Rufus against the wall within a loosely confining table-leg cage.

"Now," Ricky said. "Sit there and listen, asshole. You move, and your face will look worse than it already does." Ricky talked for several minutes. He remained standing and paced. He told Rufus about prison. He told him that Harley was still there and would be for a while. Then he told him about how Keith Tedrow had helped him and how they had accidentally found the money because they had to replace the stinking refrigerator. He finished with the truth. "And it is all your fault. Every damned bit of it. It is all your fault!" he screamed.

Rufus tried to regain control by reminding Ricky of times past. "Ricky, this is Rufus talking to you. I raised you. I protected you. I fed you. I sent you to school. Everything you have is because of me." Perhaps, if he'd stopped there, the reminder of his lukewarm brotherly love might have worked, but he didn't. He grasped the edge of the chair and screamed, "Do you fuckin' know who you are talking to? You are nothing but an ungrateful, schoolboy prick."

Ricky shoved the upturned table aside, clearing the way for his outraged and liberated response. He stood directly in front of Rufus and slapped him hard across the left side of his face. Rufus's head snapped sharply to his right and bounced back, spewing blood. His nose bled again, and Ricky felt Rufus's dominance evaporate in the anger-purified air. Rufus was shocked into silence.

Ricky walked to the sink, dampened the dishcloth, and tossed it at Rufus. It hit him in the chest and fell in his lap. Rufus picked it up and held it to his nose. Ricky placed another chair, back first, in front his dazed and bleeding brother. He straddled the chair and leaned in, close to Rufus's face.

"What happened to your face. You look like crap," Ricky said. "I don't know."

"Musta' been drunk, right?"

"I guess. What difference does it make?" Rufus was depleted, but defiant.

"You don't remember, do you? Let's see if you remember this: Tell me why you ditched me. Why'd you leave me there on that road alone, Rufus?"

Rufus took a deep breath and twisted his blood-smudged face into a contemptuous smirk, anticipating the sweet satisfaction of his hateful answer. "Simple. You're a pussy, that's why. You're too goddamned friendly. When you're runnin' from the law, you can't make friends with every swingin' dick that comes along. That's what you'da done, and they'da caught us sure as shit. Besides, you woulda hated it. Bein' a fugitive means layin' low and stayin' mean. That ain't your style now is it, little brother?" Rufus paused, sneered, and then spat out his words one at a time. "I did you a favor, you ungrateful little prick!"

Any measure of indecision dissolved in Ricky's angry resolve. "It's my turn to do you a favor, Rufus. You tired of running?"

"I ain't going to jail if that's what you mean," Rufus said.

Ricky stood, turned the table upright and moved it to its proper place in front of the sink. Rufus started to stand. Ricky spun around and pushed him back down in the chair. "Sit down and shut up," he said. Then he stepped to the kitchen counter, removed a butcher knife from a drawer, and cut the cord off the toaster. "Hold your hands out in front of you, Rufus."

"Fuck you, little brother."

"Hold out your hands! Do it now!"

Rufus held his fisted hands in front of him and lunged forward in an awkward, off-balance charge intended to overpower his physically superior brother. Ricky's knee thrust squarely into Rufus's chest and stopped him. Rufus fell backward into the chair, gasping for breath, as Ricky quickly bound his hands before him with the severed cord. He forced Rufus to stand, grabbed the chair, and marched him to the barn.

Deputized

Keith awoke from a sound sleep when the phone rang at 12:30 a.m. Somehow, he knew it was Ricky even before he answered.

"Hello," Keith answered.

"Keith, Rufus is here. I got him tied up in the barn," Ricky blurted.

Keith was silent as he swung his feet out of bed and sorted out what he had just heard.

"You still there, Keith?"

"Yes, yes, I'm here, Ricky. Repeat what you just said."

"I said Rufus is here. He just showed up out of nowhere. I got him tied up in the barn."

"He's tied up?"

"Yeah, he got madder 'en hell when he seen his money was gone. I explained how his money was safe in the bank, but he wouldn't listen. He just got madder and madder. I had to do somethin'."

"So, you tied him up? Did you hurt him?"

"Nah. His nose is bleeding a little. But he's okay. His face was all beat up when he got here. Don't know what happened to him. It wasn't my doin'. He was screaming curse words at me, so I slapped him once, then knocked the wind out of him when he came at me. That's all I did. What should I do now?"

"Ricky, how long can you hold him? Is he absolutely secure?"

"He ain't goin' no place. He's tied up good. I thought about givin' him his money and turnin' him loose. Tell him if he ever comes back, I'd turn him in. Course, that'd mean keepin' him tied up till tomorrow, when I can get the money."

"Ricky, that's the last thing you want to do. He is a wanted man. If you help him in any way, you'd be in trouble. You're still on parole, you know. You'd go back to jail. You don't want that, do you?"

"No!"

"You must turn him in. I know he's your brother, Ricky. But he's also the reason for all your problems."

"That's what I told him," Ricky said.

"You owe him nothing. Ricky, lockin' him up, is best for him. It'd be best for you too. He'd be out of your hair for a long, long time. If you turn him loose, he'll be back to muck up your life, again and again. I guarantee it. Yes, he's your brother, but he's also an evil man who is capable of terrible things, like kidnapping Jimmy. You must turn him in."

"Who do I call?"

"Leave that to me, Ricky. You just sit tight and make damned sure he's secured. I'll get somebody up there as fast as I can. But whatever you do. Don't let him go. Keep him tied up."

Keith's wife was wide awake. "What's going on, Keith?" she asked as she sat up in bed.

"Rufus is back. I'll tell you more in a minute,"

Keith hurried down the hall toward the kitchen junk drawer where he stashed his collection of seldom-used business cards. Janson's and Adam's cards topped the stack. Adam's included a home number. Jason's didn't. He called Adam.

Adam noticed the time on the bedside clock radio as he answered the phone. It was ten until one.

"Adam. This is Keith Tedrow. I need your help. Are you awake enough to talk?"

"Yeah, I guess so."

"Rufus is back at the Hudson farm. Ricky has him tied up in the barn. We've got to get someone up there to arrest him. I'm going up there as soon as we hang up, just to protect Ricky. Please call someone with authority to put this guy away."

Now fully awake, Adam repeated what he'd heard. "Rufus is back and being held captive in Hudson's barn by Ricky. Is that right?"

"Right."

"Why didn't you call the police?"

"I didn't have a number handy, and, honestly, I was afraid I'd get Deputy Hargrove, and he doesn't inspire confidence, if you know what I mean."

"Yeah, I know what you mean. I'll call Sheriff Bartlow. But don't be surprised if Hargrove leads the charge. He's closest to you. I'll call you back when we have a plan. I have your number."

Adam felt Connie sit up beside him. "Sounds like another Hudson episode."

"Yep," he said, then back to the phone, "Keith, be damned careful. Rufus is an evil man. I'll call you as soon as I can."

"Adam, I'll wait here for fifteen minutes. After that, I'm leaving for the Hudson's. Talk soon." Keith hung up.

Adam quickly learned that making phone calls after midnight is the best way to do business. People are where they should be and, chances are, they will answer the phone themselves. He talked to Sheriff Bartlow and Jason Salisbury and called Keith back inside of twelve minutes. When he spoke to Sheriff Bartlow, he surprised himself. He asked if he could ride along with him during his early-morning trip to Snyder. His emotional investment in the case trumped his easy-going ways and revealed a latent and alluring fondness for the hunt. He was an unofficial team member, but he'd been part of the chase and should be part of the capture. He was surprised when Sheriff Bartlow said yes.

"But I'll have to deputize you if you're going be in the car with a prisoner. If that don't bother you, come ahead on. I'd enjoy the company."

"Deputize?"

"Repeat after me, 'I promise to do everything that Sheriff Bartlow asks me to do. So, help me, God.' "

Adam repeated the pledge and smiled.

"Great, I'll give you a badge when I pick you up at one thirty. Can't give you a gun, but I'll give you a can of mace or a billy. Doubt you'll need them."

"Okay, see ya when you get here."

Adam sat on the edge of the bed for a moment before he dressed. Carrying a weapon of any kind was a new thought for Adam. It fostered nervous clarity about the objective of the early-morning drive to Snyder. Still, he wanted to go. "Connie, I'm going back to Snyder tonight with Sheriff Bartlow. They've captured Rufus."

She was quiet for a long moment. Then she said, "I won't ask why. Do be careful."

"You know I will," Adam answered, and he remembered her wisdom. There is a big difference between chasing dangerous weeds and chasing dangerous men. He decided the can of mace would allow him to keep his distance from Rufus.

Sheriff Bartlow arrived on time. Before he arrived, Adam called Hubert St. John to tell him what was happening. The plan was in place.

Deputy Hargrove would immediately drive to the Hudson farm, connect with Keith Tedrow, and formally arrest Rufus. He would take his prisoner to the holding cell behind the Shell station in downtown Snyder. Sheriff Bartlow and Adam would drive to Snyder and pick up the prisoner and bring him back to Spring Valley for eventual arraignment.

Deputy Hargrove pulled into the Hudson's yard only seconds behind Keith. Keith saw Hargrove's headlights behind him, parked in front of the barn, and waited for Hargrove to join him. The two men walked toward a sliver of light escaping from the partially open barn door. Hargrove reached the door first but didn't enter. He stopped short of open door and signaled Keith to delay his entry. He yelled, "Ricky, are you in there?"

"I'm here," Ricky answered.

"We're coming in."

"Come ahead," Ricky answered.

The barn had electricity, but its four sixty-watt bulbs in caged fixtures mounted high on each wall of the large room did little more than turn darkness into hazy incandescent dusk. But it was enough light to see Rufus lashed to the barn's center beam. He was seated in a kitchen chair. His hands were in his lap, still tied with the toaster cord. A braided hemp rope encircled him, the chair, and the beam six times before it was tied off behind him. Ricky had done his job well.

Keith looked at Rufus, smiled at Ricky, then allowed his eyes to climb the ladder to the hayloft where Jimmy had been held captive. Sadness enveloped him and quickly became anger. It was in his gut, between his eyes, and in his throat. For that moment, Keith saw Rufus Hudson as Lucifer himself. Keith's emotional detour was abruptly halted as Deputy Hargrove took charge with a noticeable measure of flaunted authority.

"Hello, Rufus," Hargrove said in a loud and artificially friendly voice. He shined his flashlight in Rufus's face, down to his hands, and finally to his feet. "Let's start down here, should we?" Hargrove looked up at Rufus in a mock invitation for Rufus's approval. He tossed a set of leg irons on the floor before him. They were on and locked in seconds. He replaced the toaster cord with handcuffs, stepped back and Mirandized his prisoner. "Okay, Ricky, want to undo that rope for me?"

Ricky untied his bruised and weary brother.

"Okay, Rufus. Stand up. You ready to take a little ride?" Hargrove asked.

Rufus stood slowly, stretched his neck, and rotated his shoulders. Then he spoke, "I gotta piss. Can you give me time enough to take a piss?"

"Sure. Rather have you do it here than in the car. Let's take it outside. Hey, Keith, slide that door open, will you?"

Keith pushed the single-track barn door wide open. Darkness consumed most of the soft light that escaped through the open door, leaving only enough to partially illuminate the cars and a short section of the barn wall on each side of the open door.

"Okay, Rufus. Let's go. We're going to walk outside and turn right. You'll stay in the light and find a spot along the wall and do your thing," Hargrove said.

Hargrove held tight to Rufus's left shoulder and arm, guiding him toward the door. Rufus shuffled across the dirt floor and through the door, hobbled by the eighteen inches of chain that dragged between his ankles. Hargrove steered him to the right and toward the barn wall, face first. Then stepped back.

"Okay, Rufus, pretend the barn's on fire and put it out," the deputy said.

His water ran for almost a minute, dampening the wall and soil around him. When it stopped, Rufus was relieved, but unstable. He wobbled and thrust his cuffed hands against the wall to maintain his balance.

"Come on, Rufus. Put yourself away, and let's go. Do you need a flashlight to find it?" Hargrove asked.

Rufus froze, stabilized by his two-handed lean against the barn wall. Hargrove walked close behind him and placed an authoritative hand on his right shoulder. The shackle chain was just long enough to allow Rufus to raise his right foot and slam his booted heel into Hargrove's instep. Hargrove screamed and went to a knee for a split second. He bounced up fast and thrust his full weight into Rufus's back. Rufus hit the wall face first and slid down slowly to the moist soil beneath him. Hargrove grabbed him by his overall suspenders and pulled him back to dry ground. Rufus lay on his back, unconscious and bleeding from his nose.

When Sheriff Bartlow and Adam walked into the cinderblock confinement shed behind the Shell station, they found Deputy Hargrove seated with his right shoe off. His throbbing foot was wrapped in ice and elevated on a milk crate, and the left pocket on his blood-stained shirt flopped free of its stitching. Rufus slept in the cell behind him.

"Holy crap, Hargrove. What the hell happened to you? Old Rufus give you some trouble, did he?" Bartlow asked.

"Nothin' I couldn't handle," Hargrove said. "He is one mean sumbitch; I'll tell you that." He described the pissing incident in great detail. Then he added, "Don't worry. The blood on my shirt is all his, not mine. Got it all over me as I loaded his unconscious ass into the car. Plus, caught my badge on the damned door handle and ripped the pocked off my shirt. Sooner you get that evil bastard out of here, the happier I'll be."

"Did ya read him his rights?" asked the Sheriff.

"Sure did, just before we untied him."

"Get that foot over to Doc Olsen's tomorrow, will ya? Make sure it ain't broke. Let me know what you find out. Sorry, you got banged up. But, nice work, Hargrove. You done good."

Deputy Hargrove beamed.

Sheriff Bartlow and Adam moved groggy Rufus to the back seat of the cruiser without incident, although Rufus did awaken as Bartlow laced a chain through his shackles and handcuffs and attached it to the D-ring protruding from the floor. Rufus stared at his manacled hands, looked up, and saw Adam seated in the front seat.

"Well, I'll be damned. If it ain't the weed man. Little outa your league, ain't ya? I didn't figure you'd have guts enough to be here for the rough stuff."

Adam turned around slowly, looked at wounded Rufus, and smiled. "Glad you woke up, Rufus. I been meanin' to talk to you about the nasty stand of noxious weeds you got on your farm. You ever do anything about 'em?"

"Kiss my ass, Thompson."

Adam knew it didn't take much to make Rufus angry. Even so, doing it was fun. He faced forward as Bartlow turned on his headlights and pulled into the darkness of Highway 72 toward Spring Valley. Rufus slept again as they drove.

"So far, so good. What do you think, Deputy Thompson? Bein' a lawman seems to agree with you," Sheriff Bartlow kidded.

Adam chuckled at the mention of his new and dubious title. "Been pretty smooth sailing, hasn't it? I gotta say, it looked like Hargrove earned his money tonight."

"Yes, sir. I'll bet this is a night the superdep won't forget."

"Superdep?" Adam asked.

"That's what some of us call him . . . behind his back, of course. You know how he gets: all puffed up about bein' a deputy. Not sure why, and it ain't my job to know. My job's to make sure he gets the job done, and he usually does. I know his fondness of overplayin' his importance is aggravatin' at times. But I guarantee ya, come hell or high water, Rufus Hudson was going to sleep behind bars tonight if Deputy Hargrove had anything to say about it."

"Remind me to thank him for a job well done," Adam said.

"He'll appreciate that. But, by the looks of Rufus I think he got the worst of it. You know, things might have turned out different for him if he hadn't made such a big mistake."

"Mistake? You mean coming home to get his money?"

"No, he stepped on Hargrove's spit-shined shoe."

Both men laughed. Adam laughed loudest.

23

Thirty Glorious Minutes

RUFUS WAS SENTENCED TO ten years in the State Penitentiary for kidnapping and interstate flight. He plead innocent, but his Omaha lawyer was out of his depth. This was not a trial for a soon-forgotten misdemeanor. It was a kidnapping trial without loopholes or technical miscues. The defense attorney was totally outmatched by Jason Salisbury and the cadre of witnesses who testified against Rufus, who sat at the defendant's table clean shaven and uncomfortable in a crisp white shirt and a clip-on necktie.

Adam, Sheriff Bartlow, Jimmy Tedrow, and Ricky Hudson all testified. Adam's retelling of the note in the back-window dust, complete with photo and matching fingerprints, set the stage. Jimmy explained his captivity in gripping detail and described Rufus as a mean and angry man. But Ricky's testimony was the most damning. He spoke slowly and confidently, while looking at his brother square in the eyes. He explained Rufus's volatile and unpredictable temperament and his singular involvement in the kidnapping. "It was wrong, what he done. I told him so. Even Harley agreed with me. But Rufus just wouldn't listen. We argued with him for two days. When he finally came around, it was too late. The deed was done, and we was on the run. The plan to get Jimmy home was mine. Rufus agreed to it only because keeping Jimmy would've been trouble that didn't end, and he knew it."

Salisbury pressed Ricky to help him understand why the kidnapping occurred in the first place. "Why would someone commit such a crime just out of the blue?" he asked. "Kidnapping doesn't seem to be a spur-of-the-moment decision, does it?"

"That's just the way Rufus is," Ricky answered. "He gets drunk and gets angry and just does stuff. Reckless stuff. Most of the time, he gets away with it. This time he didn't."

Rufus's incarceration overlapped Harley's by about two weeks. They never saw one another while they were imprisoned and only one time after Harley was released. Ricky and Harley visited Rufus at the state prison in Lincoln about a month after Harley was freed. Ricky planned the visit primarily for Harley, although he hoped the visit would give each of them some sense of closure to the painful kidnapping saga.

They sat at a guarded table in the vacant visitation room: Rufus on one side, his brothers on the other. An ever-present guard stood against the wall near the door. Harley was delighted to see his older brother. However, his first words belied his happiness. He asked, "Rufus, what happened to your nose?"

"Ask your little brother," Rufus said. His healed nose lay flat and crooked between his bloated cheeks. "He knows all about it."

The three brothers sat silent for an uncomfortable moment. Rufus, thinking he had re-established family dominance with a single verbal punch, retreated to the high ground of feigned brotherly kindness. "Been awhile since we seen them presidents, hasn't it, Harley? That was fun, wasn't it?"

"Yeah, never seen anything like it. Maybe we can do it again."

"Maybe so. Maybe so," Rufus answered.

"They said you went to Montana after that," Ricky said. "What did you do up there all that time?"

"Got a job. Rented a nice place. Made some friends. Hated to leave, but I ran out of money and had to come home. Unfortunately, you took my money."

"Told ya, your money is untouched and in a safe place." Ricky ran the fingers of his right hand inside his shirt collar and retrieved the chain, which held the deposit box key. He let the key dangle over his index finger. "See this key. This here's the key to the bank box. Your money is safe." Ricky meant to reassure. What Rufus heard was a mean-spirited taunt.

Then Ricky said something he regretted. "When I first seen ya there at the house, you was awful beat up. Always wondered what happened to ya. Maybe you ran out of friends, as well as money?"

Rufus couldn't talk about his last night in Stampede, even if he wanted to. There was a troubling hole in his memory where his Stampede Tavern skirmish with Bobby and Buck should have been. The void worried him, but he put it to good use. He back filled it with combustible loathing, and Ricky's comment lit the short fuse. Rufus exploded. His bottom came off the chair as he leaned across the table and screamed in Ricky's face. "I'll tell ya when I ran out of friends. When I got home and you called the law on me. That's when, you ungrateful little, shit-faced traitor."

The guard took three, quick steps forward from his spot on the wall. Rufus saw him coming and settled back in his chair, red faced and seething. The guard relaxed but remained three steps closer to the table.

"I had no choice," Ricky said quietly.

"Bull shit!" Rufus snarled, still angry but quieter. "You had a choice. Friends or family, that was your choice. You chose your phony-assed friends."

Trading barbs with Rufus was not Ricky's goal. He planned the meeting for Harley's benefit, and it was clear that the family reunion would remain a bitter confrontation if he remained at the table. He looked at the guard and nodded, told Harley he'd be right outside, and left the room. Harley and Rufus talked for another twenty minutes.

In spite of Rufus's outburst, the meeting was successful, although the upshot was different for each man. Harley was pleased to see Rufus. He looked forward seeing him again. Ricky affirmed his freedom; not a trace of subservience to his domineering big brother remained. Rufus revisited happiness. He sat across from his brothers feeling powerful, entitled and vindictively cheerful. It was like old times. For thirty glorious minutes he was, once again, the family kingpin.

The meeting rekindled his need to dominate. Unfortunately, Rufus's renewed desire to rule was not well received by his fellow inmates, especially after he befriended a deep thinker who belonged to somebody else. Rufus was stabbed to death in the exercise yard just two months after his incarceration.

24

Ice-Cream Truth

IT WAS A GORGEOUS, early-October Sunday. The entire family gathered at Mike's house after church for a cookout. Scott and Sally kept Sally's pregnancy secret so they could be face to face with Adam and Connie when they made the announcement. A family gathering on Mike's spacious deck was a perfect time and place to share their good news. After hamburgers, baked beans, and potato salad, Mike beat them to the punch with an announcement of his own.

"Who wants homemade ice cream?" Mike asked as he pulled the ice-cream coated paddles from the freezer canister. "Come and get it!"

"I do, I do, I do!" Six-year-old William shouted. He was first in line with his ice-cream dish in hand. His little sister was close behind. With the kids and the adults all served, Scott scooted back from the picnic table, stood, and theatrically cleared his throat. Once assured of everyone's attention, he smiled and said, "After watching Mike announce his ice cream, I was reminded that, as the younger brother, it is high time for me share the limelight. While it is true that there is nothing more delicious than Mike's homemade ice cream, it is also true that there is nothing more important to Sally and me than this family. That's why we've decided to add to it. We're pregnant. There will be a new Thompson grandchild in March."

Connie sat next to Sally. Her hushed giggle became a delighted squeal, as she jumped to her feet and embraced Sally. Sally remained seated and pushed her ice-cream dish forward, away from the commotion of Connie's enthusiastic squeeze. Sally smiled broadly.

"I knew it. I knew it, I knew it! What wonderful news!" Connie said. "Dad and I were just wondering about this day, and here it is!"

Adam leaned back, bringing the front legs of his molded plastic chair off the deck floor. He teetered once and then slid forward into a perfect four-point landing, which included a two-handed slap on the picnic table and a huge grin. "What do you think about that, kids? You're going to have a cousin."

The celebration didn't cease. Sally, Molly, and Connie's delighted chatter continued as they cleared the table and went inside. Susan followed. Mike challenged William to a Frisbee toss in the backyard. Only Scott and Adam remained at the picnic table in an accidental private moment.

Everyone knew about Rufus's death, but no one mentioned it. It could have been because the kids were underfoot or because of the splendid October sunshine, which didn't invite conversations about recently departed convicts. Or, it could have been because everyone was happy to be on the other side of the Hudson debacle. Despite all that, Scott probed cautiously.

"Dad, figure you'll ever get back up to Snyder?"

"Yeah, I suppose I will. I'm bettin' it'll be a different place without Rufus."

"Amazing how one man can cause so much pain. But, as strange as it seems, I was saddened by the news of his death," Scott said.

"Me too. Kind of sucks the hope right out of victory. Rehabilitation isn't an option, is it? Curious how you can miss someone you despised."

"I hope Ricky doesn't blame himself."

"After watching him testify, I think there's little chance of that," Adam said. "I think he'll do just fine, especially with folks like Keith Tedrow in his corner. Eventually, most people in Snyder will warm to him, I'll bet. Harley, too, probably."

"You really think Ricky and Harley will be able to get out from under the Hudson brother cloud?" Scott asked.

"Without Rufus, there won't be much of a cloud. Of course, it won't happen overnight. They've been a bad-tempered trio in Snyder for a long time. Still, with Rufus gone, things should change."

"Just think. It's change that you started, Dad," Scott said.

"Nah, I didn't start it. I was an accidental part of the last chapter. Change this big starts somewhere distant and lopes along at its own pace for a long time. This one probably began when a hardscrabble father decided to let his youngest son finish school, maybe even before. Then it found its way to a kindhearted boy who secretly shared his cutting board with his unfortunate classmate and ended with Rufus's crazy decision to kidnap Jimmy.

"It all led to a long-overdue, righteous reset for Ricky. Gosh, when Ricky knocked Rufus to the floor in their kitchen that night, he must have felt a rush of freedom that surprised the hell out of him. I wasn't there, but I love thinking about it. Most times, life's moments just fold behind us into a gentle ribbon of slow-drying lava, eventually hardening into who we are. Other times they explode before us, sending molten rocks flying. They change everything. I'll bet that was such a moment for Ricky."

"In a way, Ricky's reset was Rufus's ruin," Scott said.

"It led to his arrest, not his death. Whose fault was Rufus's death?" Adam asked. "Sure wasn't Ricky's. Oh, you could blame the guy who stabbed him. More to it than that, I think. Rufus's inability to change was the blade that cut him. You'd think the good Lord would've nudged Rufus sometime along the way and told him it was time to change his ways. Maybe he did and Rufus didn't hear him. Couldn't, I guess."

Scott lifted his glass of iced tea and said, "Here's to the willingness to change."

"Here, here!" Adam said, joining the toast with his empty glass. "And to the brand-new person who will soon join our family—and to the changes that gift will require."

The screen door opened and closed softly. Four-year-old Susan returned to the deck and crawled up on her granddad's lap. Adam greeted her with a welcoming smile, which made his scar more noticeable. Susan reached up and gently passed her tiny fingers across her grandfather's dented eyebrow. He was sure she was going to ask him how he got the scar, which would have forced him to conjure up another fun-filled fib. But she didn't. She said, "Does that still hurt you, Grandpa?"

"No, it doesn't hurt. It is all healed up."

"Will it ever go away?" she asked.

Adam thought for a moment. "No, it won't go away," he said. "Scars are like that, you know. They just become part of who you are. This one's a good part, I think. Thank you for asking me."

www.ingramcontent.com/pod-product-compliance
Lightning Source LLC
Chambersburg PA
CBHW051551280626
47162CB00021B/1677